"I really don't think this is a good idea, Elena."

"Too bad then that I do." She stood on her tiptoes and brushed a kiss across his mouth. "That's only the second kiss I've ever had," she whispered against his lips. "The first was two nights ago, when you held me in your arms."

He closed his eyes. He was the only man who had ever kissed her? Didn't she realize how much she was giving him, offering him freely? Didn't she know how hurt she might be afterward? No matter what she said or promised now. She was young. Inexperienced. Innocent.

He forced his eyes open, wrapped his hands around hers and attempted to draw them away for her. "I don't want to hurt you, Elena."

"You won't."

"You don't know that. You *can't* know that, because you've never done this before."

"And when am I going to get a chance to do it, Khalil?" she asked, her honest gaze clashing with his. "I was going to give myself to a man I barely knew, for the sake of my country. That possibility has been taken away from me now. You've taken it away from me, and I think it's only fair you offer me something in return. You owe me a wedding night."

Rivals to the Crown of Kadar

Ruthless in battle, ruthless in love....

Two powerful men locked in a struggle to rule the country of their birth...

One a desert prince, once banished and shamed, the other a royal playboy cutting a swathe through the beautiful women of Europe.

Tortured by their memories of the past, these bitter enemies will use any means necessary to win...but neither expects the women who will change the course of their revenge!

Read Khalil's story in

Captured by the Sheikh

September 2014

Read Aziz's story in

Commanded by the Sheikh

October 2014

Kate Hewitt

—

Captured by the Sheikh

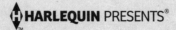
HARLEQUIN PRESENTS®

Recycling programs
for this product may
not exist in your area.

ISBN-13: 978-0-373-13274-4

CAPTURED BY THE SHEIKH

First North American Publication 2014

Printed in U.S.A.

HARLEQUIN®

™ www.Harlequin.com

All about the author...
Kate Hewitt

KATE HEWITT discovered her first Harlequin® romance novel on a trip to England when she was thirteen, and she's continued to read them ever since. She wrote her first story at the age of five, simply because her older brother had written one and she thought she could do it, too. That story was one sentence long—fortunately, they've become a bit more detailed as she's grown older.

She studied drama in college and shortly after graduation moved to New York City to pursue a career in theater. This was derailed by something far better—meeting the man of her dreams, who happened also to be her older brother's childhood friend. Ten days after their wedding they moved to England, where Kate worked a variety of different jobs—drama teacher, editorial assistant, youth worker, secretary and, finally, mother.

When her oldest daughter was one year old, Kate sold her first short story to a British magazine. Since then she has sold many stories and serials, but writing romance remains her first love—of course!

Besides writing, she enjoys reading, traveling and learning to knit—it's an ongoing process, and she's made a lot of scarves. After living in England for six years, she now resides in Connecticut with her husband, her three young children and, possibly one day, a dog.

Kate loves to hear from readers. You can contact her through her website, www.kate-hewitt.com.

Other titles by Kate Hewitt available in ebook:

A QUEEN FOR THE TAKING? *(The Diomedi Heirs)*
THE PRINCE SHE NEVER KNEW *(The Diomedi Heirs)*
HIS BRAND OF PASSION *(The Bryants: Powerful & Proud)*
IN THE HEAT OF THE SPOTLIGHT *(The Bryants: Powerful & Proud)*

CHAPTER ONE

'SOMETHING'S WRONG—'

Elena Karras, Queen of Thallia, had barely registered the voice of the royal steward behind her when a man in a dark suit, his face harsh-looking and his expression inscrutable, met her at the bottom of the steps that led from the royal jet to this bleak stretch of desert.

'Queen Elena. Welcome to Kadar.'

'Thank you.'

He bowed and then indicated one of three armoured SUVs waiting by the airstrip. 'Please accompany us to our destination,' he said, his voice clipped yet courteous. He stepped aside so she could move forward, and Elena threw back her shoulders and lifted her chin as she walked towards the waiting cars.

She hadn't expected fanfare upon her arrival to marry Sheikh Aziz al Bakir, but she supposed she'd thought she'd have a little more than a few security guards and blacked-out cars.

Then she reminded herself that Sheikh Aziz wanted to keep her arrival quiet, because of the instability within Kadar. Ever since he'd taken the throne just over a month ago there had been, according to Aziz, some minor insurgent activity. At their last meeting, he'd assured her it was taken care of, but she supposed a few security measures were a necessary precaution.

Just like the Sheikh, she needed this marriage to succeed. She barely knew the man, had only met him a few times, but she needed a husband just as he needed a wife.

Desperately.

'This way, Your Highness.'

The man who'd first greeted her had been walking beside her from the airstrip to the SUV, the desert endlessly dark all around them, the night-time air possessing a decided chill. He opened the door of the vehicle and Elena tipped her head up to the inky sky, gazing at the countless stars glittering so coldly above them.

'*Queen Elena.*'

She stiffened at the sound of the panicked voice, recognising it as that of the steward from the Kadaran royal jet. The man's earlier words belatedly registered: *something's wrong.*

She started to turn and felt a hand press into the small of her back, staying her.

'Get in the car, Your Highness.'

An icy sweat broke out between her shoulder blades. The man's voice was low and grim with purpose—not the way he'd sounded earlier, with his clipped yet courteous welcome. And she knew, with a sickening certainty, that she did not want to get in that car.

'Just a moment,' she murmured, and reached down to adjust her shoe, buy a few seconds. Her mind buzzed with panic, static she silenced by sheer force of will. She needed to *think*. Somehow something had gone wrong. Aziz's people hadn't met her as expected. This stranger had and, whoever he was, she knew she needed to get away from him. To plan an escape—and in the next few seconds.

She felt a cold sense of purpose come over her, clearing her mind even as she fought a feeling of unreality. *This was happening. Again, the worst was happening.*

She knew all about dangerous situations. She knew what it felt like to stare death in the face—and survive.

And she knew, if she got in the car, escape would become no more than a remote possibility.

She fiddled with her shoe, her mind racing. If she kicked off her heels she could sprint back to the jet. The steward was obviously loyal to Aziz; if they managed to close the door before this man came after her...

It was a better option than running into the dark desert. It was her only option.

'Your Highness.' Impatience sharpened the man's voice. His hand pressed insistently against her back. Taking a deep breath, Elena kicked off her heels and ran.

The wind streamed past her and whipped sand into her face as she streaked towards the jet. She heard a sound behind her and then a firm hand came round her waist, lifting her clear off the ground.

Even then she fought. She kicked at the solid form behind her; the man's body now felt like a stone wall. She bent forward, baring her teeth, trying to find some exposed skin to bite, anything to gain her freedom.

Her heel connected with the man's kneecap and she kicked again, harder, then hooked her leg around his and kicked the back of his knee so the man's leg buckled. They both fell to the ground.

The fall winded her but she was up within seconds, scrambling on the sand. The man sprang forward and covered her with his body, effectively trapping her under him.

'I admire your courage, Your Highness,' he said in her ear, his voice a husky murmur. 'As well as your tenacity. But I'm afraid both are misplaced.'

Elena blinked through the sand that stung her eyes and clung to her cheeks. The jet was still a hundred yards away. How far had she managed to run? Ten feet? Twenty?

The man flipped her over so she was on her back, his arms braced on either side of her head. She gazed up at him, her heart thudding against her ribs, her breath coming in little pants. He was poised above her like a panther, his eyes the bewitching amber of a cat's, his face all chiselled planes and harsh angles. Elena could feel his heat, sense his strength. This man radiated power. Authority. *Danger.*

'You would never have made it back to the plane,' he told her, his voice treacherously soft. 'And, even if you had, the men on it are loyal to me.'

'My guards—'

'Bribed.'

'The steward—'

'Powerless.'

She stared at him, trying to force down her fear. 'Who *are* you?' she choked.

He bared his teeth in a feral smile. 'I'm the future ruler of Kadar.'

In one fluid movement he rolled off her, pulling her up by a hand that had closed around her wrist like a manacle. Still holding her arm, he led her back to the cars, where two other men waited, dark-suited and blank-faced. One of them opened the rear door and with mocking courtesy her arrogant captor, whoever he really was, sketched an elaborate bow.

'After you, Your Highness.'

Elena stared at the yawning darkness of the SUV's interior. She *couldn't* get in that car. As soon as she did the doors would lock and she'd be this man's prisoner.

But she already was his prisoner, she acknowledged sickly, and she'd just blown her best bid for freedom. Perhaps if she pretended compliance now, or even fear, she'd find another opportunity for escape. She wouldn't even have to pretend all that much; terror had begun to claw at her senses.

She looked at the man who was watching her with cold amusement, as if he'd already guessed the nature of her thoughts.

'Tell me who you really are.'

'I already did, Your Highness, and you are trying my

patience. Now, get in the car.' He spoke politely enough, but Elena still felt the threat. The danger. She saw that cold, knowing amusement in the man's amber eyes, but no pity, no spark of compassion at all, and she knew she was out of options.

Swallowing hard, she got in the car.

The man slid in beside her and the doors closed, the automated lock a loud click in the taut silence. He tossed her shoes onto her lap.

'You might want those.' His voice was low, unaccented, and yet he was clearly Arabic. Kadaran. His skin was a deep bronze, his hair as dark as ink. The edge of his cheekbone looked as sharp as a blade.

Swallowing again, the taste of fear metallic on her tongue, Elena slipped them on. Her hair was a mess, one knee was scraped and the skirt of her staid navy blue suit was torn.

Taking a deep breath, she tucked her hair behind her ears and wiped the traces of sand from her face. She looked out of the window, trying to find some clue as to where they were going, but she could barely see out of the tinted glass. What she could see was nothing more than the jagged black shapes of rocks in the darkness, Kadar's infamously bleak desert terrain. It was a small country nestled on the Arabian Peninsula, its borders containing both magnificent coastline and deadly rock-strewn desert.

She sneaked a sideways glance at her captor. He sat with his hands resting lightly on his thighs, looking relaxed and assured, yet also alert. Who was he? Why had he kidnapped her?

And how was she going to get free?

Think, she told herself. Rational thought was the antidote to panic. The man must be one of the rebel insurgents Aziz had mentioned. He'd said he was the future ruler of Kadar, which meant he wanted Aziz's throne. He must have kidnapped her to prevent their marriage—unless he wasn't aware of the stipulations set out in Aziz's father's will?

Elena had only learned of them when she'd met Aziz a few weeks ago at a diplomatic function. His father, Sheikh Hashem, had just died and Aziz had made some sardonic joke about now needing a wife. Elena hadn't been sure whether to take him seriously or not, but then she'd seen a bleakness in his eyes. She'd felt it in herself.

Her Head of Council, Andreas Markos, was determined to depose her. He claimed a young, inexperienced woman such as herself was unfit to rule, and had threatened to call for a vote to abolish the monarchy at the next convening of the Thallian Council. But if she were married by then... if she had a husband and Prince Consort...then Markos couldn't argue she was unfit to rule.

And the people loved a wedding, wanted a royal marriage. She was popular with the Thallian people; it was why Markos hadn't already tried to depose her in the four turbulent years of her reign. Adding to that popularity with a royal wedding would make her position even stronger.

It was a desperate solution, but Elena had felt desperate. She loved her country, her people, and she wanted to remain their queen—for their sake, and for her father's sake, who had given his life so she could be monarch.

The next morning Elena had sent a letter to Aziz, suggesting they meet. He'd agreed and, with a candour borne of urgency, they'd laid out their respective positions. Elena needed a husband to satisfy her Council; Aziz needed to marry within six weeks of his father's death or he forfeited his title. They'd agreed to wed. They'd agreed to a convenient and loveless union that would give them the spouses they needed and children as heirs, one for Kadar, one for Thallia.

It was a mercenary approach to both marriage and parenthood and, if she'd been an ordinary woman, or even an ordinary queen, she would have wanted something different for her life. But she was a queen hanging onto her kingdom by a mere thread, and marriage to Aziz al Bakir had felt like the only way to keep clinging.

But for that to happen, she had to get married. And to get married, she had to escape.

She couldn't get out of the car, so she needed to wait. Watch. Learn her enemy.

'What is your name?' she asked. The man didn't even look at her.

'My name is Khalil.'

'Why have you taken me?'

He slid her a single, fathomless glance. 'We're almost at our destination, Your Highness. Your questions will be answered there, after we are both refreshed.'

Fine. She'd wait. She'd stay calm and in control and look for the next opportunity to gain her freedom. Even so terror caught her by the throat and held on. She'd felt this terrible, numbing fear before, as if the world were sliding by in slow motion, everything slipping away from her as she waited, frozen, disbelieving that this was actually happening...

No, this was not the same as before. She wouldn't let it be. She was queen of a country, even if her throne was all too shaky a seat. She was resourceful, courageous, *strong*.

She would get out of this. Somehow. She refused to let some rebel insurgent wreck her marriage...or end her reign as queen.

Khalil al Bakir glanced again at the woman by his side. She sat straight and tall, her chin lifted proudly, her pupils dilated with fear.

Admiration for the young queen flickered reluctantly through him. Her attempt at escape had been reckless and laughable, but also brave, and he felt an unexpected sympathy for her. He knew what it was like to feel both trapped and defiant. Hadn't he, as a boy, tried to escape from his captor, Abdul-Hafiz, as often as he could, even though he'd

known how fruitless such attempts would be? Deep in the
desert, there had been no place for a young boy to run or
hide. Yet still he'd tried, because to try was to fight, and to
fight was to remind yourself you were alive and had something to fight for. The scars on his back were testament to
his many failed attempts.

Queen Elena would have no such scars. He would not be
accused of ill-treating his guest, no matter what the frightened monarch might think. He intended to keep her for only
four days, until the six weeks had passed and Aziz would
be forced to relinquish his claim to the throne and call a national referendum to decide who the next sheikh would be.

Khalil intended to be that man.

Until that moment, when the vote had been called and
he sat on the throne that was rightfully his, he would not
rest easy. But then, he'd never rested easy, not since the
day when he'd been all of seven years old and his father
had dragged him out of his lesson with his tutor, thrown
him onto the sharp stones in front of the Kadaran palace
and spat in his face.

'*You are not my son.*'

It was the last time he'd ever seen him, his mother, or
his home.

Khalil closed his eyes against the memories that still
made his fists clench and bile rise in his throat. He would
not think of those dark days now. He would not remember the look of disgust and even hatred on the face of the
father he'd adored, or the anguished cries of his mother
as she'd been dragged away, only to die just a few months
later from a simple case of the flu because she'd been denied adequate medical care. He wouldn't think of the terror he'd felt when he'd been shoved in the back of a van
and driven to a bleak desert outpost, or the look of cruel
satisfaction on Abdul-Hafiz's face when he'd been thrown
at his feet like a sack of rubbish.

No, he wouldn't think of any of that. He'd think of the

future, the very promising future, when he, the son his father had rejected in favour of his mistress's bastard, would sit on the throne of the kingdom he'd been born to rule.

Next to him, he felt Queen Elena tremble.

Twenty taut minutes later the SUV pulled up at the makeshift camp Khalil had called home for the last six months, ever since he'd returned to Kadar. He opened the door and turned to Elena, who glared at him in challenge.

'Where have you taken me?'

He gave her a cold smile. 'Why don't you come out and see for yourself?' Without waiting for an answer, he took hold of her wrist. Her skin was soft and cold and she let out a muffled gasp as he drew her from the car.

She stumbled on a stone as she came to her feet, and as he righted her he felt her breasts brush his chest. It had been a long time since he'd felt the soft touch of a woman, and his body responded with base instinct, his loins tightening as desire flared deep inside. Her hair, so close to his face, smelled of lemons.

Firmly Khalil moved her away from him. He had no time for lust and certainly not with this woman.

His right-hand man, Assad, emerged from another vehicle. 'Your Highness.' Elena turned automatically, and Khalil smiled in grim satisfaction. Assad had been addressing him, not the unruly queen. Even though he had not officially claimed his title, those loyal to him still addressed him as if he had.

He'd been surprised and gratified at how many were loyal to him, when they had only remembered a touslehaired boy who'd been dragged crying and gibbering from the palace. Until six months ago, he had not been in Kadar since he'd been ten years old. But people remembered.

The desert tribes, bound more by tradition than the people of Siyad, had always resented Sheikh Hashem's rash decision to discard one wife for a mistress no one had liked, and a son he'd already publicly declared illegitimate.

When Khalil had returned, they'd named him sheikh of his
mother's tribe and had rallied around him as the true ruling Sheikh of Kadar.

Even so, Khalil trusted no one. Loyalties could change
on a whim. Love was capricious. He'd learned those lessons all too painfully well. The only person he trusted
now was himself.

'Queen Elena and I would like some refreshment,' he
told Assad in Arabic. 'Is there a tent prepared?'

'Yes, Your Highness.'

'You can debrief me later. For now, I'll deal with the
Queen.' He turned to Elena, whose panicked gaze was darting in every direction, her body poised for flight.

'If you are thinking of running away,' he told her calmly,
switching to English as the language they both knew, 'don't
bother. The desert stretches for hundreds of miles in every
direction, and the nearest oasis is over a day's ride by
camel. Even if you managed to leave the camp, you would
die of thirst, if not a snake or scorpion bite.'

Queen Elena glared at him and said nothing. Khalil gestured her forward. 'Come, have some refreshment, and I
will answer your questions as I promised.'

Elena hesitated and then, clearly knowing she had no
choice, she nodded and followed him across the camp.

Elena took stock of her surroundings as she walked behind Khalil. A few tents formed a rough semi-circle; she
could see some horses and camels tethered to a post under
a lean-to. The wind blew sand into her face and her hair
into her mouth.

She held her hands up to her face, tried to blink the grit
out of her eyes. Khalil pushed back the folds of the tent
and ushered her inside.

Elena took a steadying breath, trying to compose herself. The only thing she could do now was learn as much
as she could, and choose her moment well.

Khalil moved to the other side of the tent, gesturing to an elegant teakwood table and low chairs with embroidered cushions. The outside of the tent had been basic, but the interior, Elena saw as her gaze darted around, was luxurious, with silk and satin furnishings and carpets.

'Please, sit down.'

'I want answers to my questions.'

Khalil turned to face her. A small smile curved his mouth but his eyes were cold. 'Your defiance is admirable, Your Highness, but only to a certain extent. Sit.'

She knew she needed to pick her battles. Elena sat. 'Where is Sheikh Aziz?'

Irritation flashed across his chiselled features and then he gave a little shrug. 'Aziz is presumably in Siyad, waiting for you.'

'He'll be expecting me—'

'Yes,' Khalil cut her off smoothly. 'Tomorrow.'

'*Tomorrow*?'

'He received a message that you were delayed.' Khalil spread his hands, his eyes glittering with what felt like mockery. 'No one is looking for you, Your Highness. And, by the time they are, it will be too late.'

The implication was obvious, and it made her breathless with shock, her vision blurring so she reached out and grabbed the edge of the table to steady herself. *Calm*. She needed to stay calm.

She heard Khalil swear softly. 'I did not mean what you obviously think I meant.'

She looked up, her vision clearing as she gazed up at him. Even scowling he was breathtaking; everything about him was lean and graceful. Predatory. 'You mean you aren't going to kill me,' she stated flatly.

'I am neither a terrorist nor a thug.'

'Yet you kidnap a queen.'

He inclined his head. 'A necessary evil, I'm afraid.'

'I don't believe any evil is necessary,' Elena shot back.

She took another steadying breath. 'So what are you going to do with me?'

It was a question she wasn't sure she wanted answered, yet she knew ignorance was dangerous. Better to know the danger, the enemy. *Know your enemies and know yourself, and you will not be imperilled in a hundred battles.*

'I'm not going to do anything with you,' Khalil answered calmly. 'Except keep you here in, I hope, moderate comfort.'

One of the guards came with a tray of food. Elena glanced at the platter of dates and figs, the flat bread and the bowls of creamy dips, and then looked away again. She had no appetite, and in any case she would not eat with her enemy.

'Thank you, Assad,' Khalil said, and the man bowed and left.

Khalil crouched on his haunches in front of the low table where Assad had set the tray. He glanced up at Elena, those amber eyes seeming almost to glow. They really were the most extraordinary colour. With his dark hair and tawny eyes, that lean, predatory elegance, he was like a leopard, or perhaps a panther—something beautiful and terrifying. 'You must be hungry, Queen Elena.'

'I am not.'

'Then thirsty, at least. It is dangerous not to drink in the desert.'

'It is dangerous,' Elena countered, 'to drink in the presence of your enemies.'

A tiny smile tugged at the corner of his mouth and he inclined his head in acknowledgement. 'Very well, then. I shall drink first.'

She watched as he poured what looked like some kind of fruit juice from an earthen pitcher into two tall tumblers. He picked up the first and drank deeply from it, the sinuous muscles of his throat working as he swallowed.

He met her gaze over the rim of his glass, his eyes glinting in challenge.

'Satisfied?' he murmured as he lowered his glass.

Elena's throat ached with thirst and was scratchy from the sand. She needed to stay hydrated if she was going to plan an escape, so she nodded and held out her hand.

Khalil handed her the glass and she sipped the juice; it was both tart and sweet, and deliciously cool.

'Guava,' he told her. 'Have you had it before?'

'No.' Elena put the glass back down on the table. 'Now I am refreshed.' She took a deep breath. 'So you intend to keep me here in the desert—for how long?'

'A little less than a week. Four days, to be precise.'

Four days. Elena's stomach knotted. In four days the six weeks Aziz had been given to marry would be up. He would lose his right to his title, and Khalil must know that. He must be waiting for a chance to seize power.

'And then?' she asked. 'What will you do?'

'That is not your concern.'

'What will you do with me?' Elena rephrased, and Khalil sat down in a low-slung chair richly patterned with wool, regarding her with a rather sleepy consideration over the tips of his steepled fingers. Elena felt her frayed nerves start to snap.

'Let you go, of course.'

'Just like that?' She shook her head, too suspicious to feel remotely relieved. 'You'll be prosecuted.'

'I don't think so.'

'You can't just kidnap a head of state.'

'And yet I have.' He took a sip of juice, his gaze resting thoughtfully on her. 'You intrigue me, Queen Elena. I must confess, I've wondered what kind of woman Aziz would choose as his bride.'

'And are you satisfied?' she snapped. *Stupid.* Where was her calm, her control? She'd been teetering on a tightrope for her entire reign; was she really going to fall off now?

But maybe she already had.

Khalil smiled faintly. 'I am not remotely satisfied.'

His gaze held her and she saw a sudden gleam of masculine intent and awareness flicker in his eyes. To her surprise and shame, she felt an answering thrill of terror—and something else. Something that wasn't fear, but rather… anticipation. Yet, of what? She wanted nothing from this man but her freedom.

'And I won't be satisfied,' Khalil continued, 'until Aziz is no longer on the throne of Kadar and I am.'

'So you are one of the rebel insurgents Aziz mentioned.'

For a second Khalil's gaze blazed fury but then he merely inclined his head. 'So it would seem.'

'Why should you be on the throne?'

'Why should Aziz?'

'Because he is the heir.'

Khalil glanced away, his expression veiled once more. 'Do you know the history of Kadar, Your Highness?'

'I've read something of it,' she answered, although the truth was her knowledge of Kadaran history was sketchy at best. There hadn't been time for more than a crash course in the heritage of the country of her future husband.

'Did you know it was a peaceful, prosperous nation for many years—independent, even, when other countries buckled under a wider regime?'

'Yes, I did know that.' Aziz had mentioned it, because her own country was the same; a small island in the Aegean Sea between Turkey and Greece, Thallia had enjoyed nearly a thousand years of peaceful, independent rule.

And she would not be the one to end it.

'Perhaps you also know, then, that Sheikh Hashem threatened the stability of Kadar with the rather unusual terms of his will?' He turned back to her, raising his eyebrows, a little smile playing about his mouth.

Elena found her gaze quite unreasonably drawn to that mouth, to those surprisingly lush and sculpted lips. She forced herself to look upwards and met Khalil's enquiring gaze. There was no point, she decided, in feigning ignorance. 'Yes, I am well aware of the old Sheikh's stipulation. It's why I am here to marry Sheikh Aziz.'

'Not a love match, then?' Khalil queried sardonically and Elena stiffened.

'I don't believe that is any of your business.'

'Considering you are here at my behest, I believe it is.'

She pursed her lips and said nothing. The Kadaran people believed it was a love match, although neither she nor Aziz had said as much. People believed what they wanted to believe, Elena knew, and the public liked the idea of a royal fairy-tale. If it helped to stabilise their countries, then so be it. She could go along with a little play-acting. But she wasn't about to admit that to Khalil.

'Pleading the fifth, I see,' Khalil said softly. 'I grew up in America, you know. I am not the barbarian you seem to think I am.'

She folded her arms. 'You have yet to show me otherwise.'

'Have I not? Yet here you are, in a comfortable chair, offered refreshment. Though I am sorry you hurt yourself.' He gestured to her scraped knee, all solicitude. 'Let me get you a plaster.'

'I don't need one.'

'Such abrasions can easily become infected in the desert. A grain of sand lodges in the cut and, the next thing you know, it's gone septic.' He leaned forward, and for a moment the harshness of his face, the coldness in his eyes, was replaced by something that almost looked like gentleness. 'Don't be stupid, Your Highness. God knows I understand the need to fight, but you are wasting your energy arguing with me over such small matters.'

She swallowed, knowing he was right, and hating it. It was petty and childish to refuse medical care, not to mention stupid as he'd said. She nodded and Khalil rose from his chair. She watched as he strode to the entrance of the tent and spoke to one of the guards waiting outside.

Elena remained seated, her fists clenched in her lap, her heart beating hard. A few minutes later Khalil returned to the table with a cloth folded over his arm, a basin of water in one hand and a tube of ointment in the other.

'Here we are.'

To her shock he knelt in front of her and Elena pressed back in her chair. 'I can do it myself.'

He glanced up at her, his eyes gleaming. 'But then you would deny me the pleasure.'

Her breath came out in a rush and she remained rigid as he gently lifted the hem of her skirt over her knee. His fingers barely brushed her leg and yet she felt as if she'd been electrocuted, her whole body jolting with sensation. Carefully Khalil dampened the cloth and then dabbed the scrape on her knee.

'Besides,' he murmured, 'you might miss some sand, and I would hate to be accused of mistreating you.'

Elena didn't answer. She couldn't speak, could barely breathe. Every atom of her being was focused on the gentle touch of this man, his fingers sliding over her knee with a precision that wasn't sensual, not remotely, yet…

She took a careful breath and stared at the top of his head, his hair ink-black and cut very short. She wondered if it would feel soft or bristly, and then jerked her mind back to her predicament. What on earth was she doing, thinking about his hair, reacting to his hands on her skin? This man was her *enemy*. The last thing, the *very* last thing, she should do was feel anything for him, even something as basic as physical desire.

His hand tightened on her knee and everything inside Elena flared to life.

'I think that's fine,' she said stiffly, and tried to draw her leg away from Khalil's hand.

He held up the tube of ointment. 'Antiseptic cream. Very important.'

Gritting her teeth, she remained still while he squeezed some cream onto his fingers and then smoothed it over the cut on her knee. It stung a little, but far more painful was the kick of attraction she felt at the languorous touch of his fingers on her sensitised skin.

It was just her body's basic physical reaction, she told herself as he rubbed circles on her knee with his thumb and her insides tightened. She'd never experienced it like this before, but then she was inexperienced in the ways of men and women. In any case, there was nothing she could do about it, so she'd ignore it. Ignore the sparks that scattered across her skin and the plunging deep in her belly. Attraction was irrelevant; she would never act on it nor allow it to cloud her judgement.

Escape from this man and his plans to ruin her marriage was her only goal now. Her only desire.

CHAPTER TWO

KHALIL FELT ELENA'S body tense beneath his touch and wondered why he had chosen to clean the cut himself. The answer, of course, was irritatingly obvious: because he'd wanted to touch her. Because, for a moment, desire had overridden sense.

Her skin, Khalil thought, was as soft as silk. When had he last touched a woman's skin? Seven years in the French Foreign Legion had given him more than a taste of abstinence.

Of course, the last woman he should ever think about as a lover was Queen Elena, Aziz's intended bride. He had no intention of complicating what was already a very delicate diplomatic manoeuvre.

Kidnapping a head of state was a calculated risk, and one he'd had to take. The only way to force Aziz to call a national referendum was for him to lose his right to the throne, and the only way for that to happen was to prevent his marriage.

His father's will, Khalil mused, had been a ridiculous piece of legal architecture that showed him for the brutal dictator he truly had been. Had he wanted to punish both his sons? Or had he, in the last days of his life, actually regretted his treatment of his first-born? Khalil would never know. But he would take the opportunity his father's strange will offered him to seize the power that was rightfully his.

'There you are.' Khalil smoothed her skirt over her knee, felt her tense body relax only slightly as he eased back. 'I see your skirt is torn. My apologies. You will be provided with new clothes.'

She stared at him, studying him as you would a specimen or, rather, an enemy: looking for weaknesses. She wouldn't find any, but Khalil took the opportunity to gaze back at her. She was lovely, her skin like golden cream, her heavy-lidded eyes grey with tiny gold flecks. Her hair was thick and dark and gleamed in the candlelight, even though it was tangled and gritty with sand.

His gaze dropped to her lips, lush, pink and perfect. Kissable. There was that desire again, flaring deep inside him, demanding satisfaction. Khalil stood up. 'You must be hungry, Your Highness. You should eat.'

'I'm not hungry.'

'Suit yourself.' He took a piece of bread and tore off a bit to chew. Sitting across from her, he studied her once more. 'I am curious as to why you agreed to marry Aziz.' He cocked his head. 'Not wealth, as Thallia is a prosperous enough country. Not power, since you are already a queen. And we know it isn't for love.'

'Maybe it is.' Her voice was low, pleasingly husky. She met his gaze unflinchingly but he heard her breath hitch and Khalil smiled.

'I don't think so, Your Highness. I think you married him because you need something, and I'm wondering what it is. Your people love you. Your country is stable.' He spread his hands, raised his eyebrows. 'What would induce you to marry a pretender?'

'I think you are the pretender, Khalil.'

'You're not the only one, alas. But you will be proved wrong.'

Her grey-gold gaze swept over him. 'You genuinely believe you have a claim to the throne.'

His stomach knotted. 'I know I do.'

'How can that be? Aziz is Sheikh Hashem's only son.'

Even though he'd long been used to such an assumption, her words poured acid on an open wound. A familiar fury rose up in him, a howl of outrage he forced back down. He smiled coldly at this woman whose careless questions tore open the barely healed scars of his past. 'Perhaps you need to brush up on your Kadaran history. You will have plenty of time for leisure reading during your stay in the desert.' Although he knew she wouldn't find the truth in any books. His father had done his best to erase Khalil's existence from history.

She stared up at him unblinkingly. 'And if I do not wish to stay in the desert?'

'Your presence here, I'm afraid, is non-negotiable. But rest assured, you will be afforded every comfort.'

Elena licked her lips, an innocent movement that still caused a hard kick of lust he instantly suppressed. Queen Elena was a beautiful woman; his body, long deprived of sensual pleasures, was bound to react. It didn't mean he was going to do anything about it.

Perhaps the most attractive thing about her, though, was not her looks but her presence. Even though he knew she had to be frightened, she sat tall and proud, her grey eyes glinting challenge. He admired her determination to be strong; he shared it. Never surrender, not even when the whole world seemed to be against you, every fist raised, every lip curled in a sneer.

Had she faced opposition and hardship? She had, he knew, suffered tragedy. She'd taken the throne at nineteen years of age, when her parents had died in a terrorist bombing. She was only twenty-three now and, though she looked very young, she seemed older in her bearing, somehow. In her confidence.

She rose from her seat, every inch the elegant queen. 'You cannot keep me here.'

He smiled; he almost felt sorry for her. 'You'll find that I can.'

'Aziz will send someone to fetch me. People will be looking.'

'Tomorrow. By that time any tracks in the desert, any evidence of where you've gone, will have vanished.' He glanced towards the tent flap, which rustled in the wind. 'It sounds as if a storm is brewing.'

Elena shook her head slowly. 'How did you manage it? To get a false message to him, convince the pilot to land somewhere else?'

'Not everyone is loyal to Aziz. In fact, few are outside of Siyad. You know he has not been in the country for more than a few days at a time since he was a boy?'

'I know he is very popular in the courts of Europe.'

'You mean the country clubs. The gentleman playboy is not so popular here.'

Elena's eyes flashed gold. 'That's a ridiculous nickname, given to him by the tabloids.'

Khalil shrugged. 'And yet it stuck.' Aziz, the playboy of Europe, who spent his time at parties and on polo fields. He ran a business too, Khalil knew; he'd started up some financial venture that was successful, if just an excuse for him to party his way through Europe and avoid the country of his birth.

Aziz didn't even *care* about Kadar, Khalil thought with a familiar spike of bitterness. He didn't deserve to rule, even if he hadn't been a bastard son.

'No matter what you think of Aziz, you can't just kidnap a queen,' Elena stated, her chin jutting out defiantly. 'You'd be wise to cut your losses, Khalil, and free me now. I won't press charges.'

Khalil suppressed a laugh of genuine amusement. 'How generous of you.'

'You don't want to face a tribunal,' she insisted. 'How can you become Sheikh if you've committed a crime?

Caused an international incident? You will be called to account.'

'You'll find that is not how things are done in my country.'

'My country, then,' she snapped. 'Do you think my Council, my country, will allow its queen to be kidnapped?'

He shrugged. 'You were merely detained, Your Highness, as a necessary measure. And, since Aziz is a pretender to the throne, you should be grateful that I am preventing a marriage you would undoubtedly regret.'

'Grateful!' Her eyes sparked with anger. 'What if your plan fails?'

He smiled coldly. 'I do not consider failure a possibility.'

She shook her head slowly, her eyes like two grey-gold pools, reminding him of a sunset reflected on water. 'You can't do this. People don't— World leaders don't do this!'

'Things are different here.'

'Not that different, surely?' She shook her head again. 'You're mad.'

Fury surged again and he took a deep, even breath. 'No, Your Highness, I am not mad. Just determined. Now, it is late and I think you should go to your quarters. You will have a private tent here and, as I said before, every comfort possible.' He bared his teeth in a smile. 'Enjoy your stay in Kadar.'

Elena paced the quarters of the elegant tent Assad had escorted her to an hour ago. Khalil had been right when he'd said he'd give her every possible comfort: the spacious tent had a wide double bed on its own wooden dais, the soft mattress piled high with silk and satin covers and pillows. There were also several teak chairs and a bureau for clothes she didn't even have.

Had they brought her luggage from the jet? She doubted it. Not that she'd even brought much to Kadar. She'd only been intending to stay for three days: a quiet ceremony, a quick honeymoon and then a return to Thallia to introduce Aziz to her people.

And now none of it would happen. Unless someone rescued her or she managed to escape, prospects she deemed quite unlikely, her marriage to Aziz would not take place. If he did not marry within the six weeks, he would be forced to relinquish his claim to the throne. He wouldn't need her then, but unfortunately she still needed him.

Still needed a husband, a Prince Consort, and before the convening of the Council next month.

Elena sank onto an embroidered chair and dropped her head into her hands. Even now she couldn't believe she was here, that she'd actually been *kidnapped*.

Yet why shouldn't she believe it? Hadn't the worst in her life happened before? For a second she remembered the sound of the explosion ringing in her ears, the terrible weight of her father's lifeless body on top of hers.

And, even after that awful day, from the moment she'd taken the throne she'd been dogged by disaster, teetering on the precipice of ruin. Led by Markos, the stuffy, sanctimonious men of the Thallian Council had sought to discredit and even disown her. They didn't want a single young woman as ruler of Thallia. They didn't want *her*.

She'd spent so much time trying to prove herself to the men of her Council who questioned her every action, doubted her every word. Who assumed she was flighty, silly and irresponsible, all because of one foolish mistake made when she'd been just nineteen and overwhelmed by grief and loneliness.

Nearly four years on, all the good she'd done for her country—all the appearances she'd made, the charities she'd supported and the bills she'd helped draft—counted for nothing. At least, not in Markos's eyes. And the rest of the Council would be led by him, even in this day and age. Thallia was a traditional country. They wanted a man as their head of state.

Tears pricked under her lids and she blinked them back furiously. She wasn't a little girl, to cry over a cut knee. She was a woman, a woman who'd had to prove she possessed the power and strength of a man for four endless, stormy years.

It couldn't end now like this, just because some crazed rebel had decided he was the rightful heir to the throne.

Except, Elena had to acknowledge, Khalil hadn't seemed crazed. He'd been coldly composed, utterly assured. Yet how could he be the rightful heir? And did he really think he could snatch the throne from under Aziz's nose? When she didn't show up in Siyad, when the Kadaran diplomat who had accompanied her sounded the alarm, Aziz would come looking. And he'd find her, because he was as desperate as she was.

Although, considering she was being held captive in the middle of the desert, perhaps she was now a little more desperate than Aziz.

He could, she realised with a terrible, sinking sensation, find another willing bride. Why shouldn't he? They'd met only a handful of times. The marriage had been her idea. He could still find someone else, although he'd have to do it pretty quickly.

Had Khalil thought of that? What was preventing Aziz from just grabbing some random woman and marrying her to fulfil the terms of his father's will?

Elena rose from the chair and once more restlessly paced the elegant confines of her tent. Outside the night was dark, the only sound the sweep of the sand and the low nickering of the tethered horses.

She *had* to talk to Khalil again and convince him to release her. That was her best chance.

Filled with grim determination, Elena whirled around and stalked to the opening of her tent, pulled the cloth aside and stepped out into the desert night, only to have two guards step quickly in front of her, their bodies as impenetrable as a brick wall. She gazed at their blank faces, at the rifles strapped to their chests, and lifted her chin.

'I want to speak to Khalil.'

'He is occupied, Your Highness.' The guard's voice was both bland and implacable; he didn't move.

'With something more important than securing the throne?' she shot back. The wind blew her hair about her face and impatiently she shoved it back. 'I have information he'll want to hear,' she stated firmly. 'Information that will affect his—his intentions.'

The two guards stared at her impassively, utterly unmoved by her argument. 'Please return to the tent, Your Highness,' one of them said flatly. 'The wind is rising.'

'Tell Khalil he needs to speak to me,' she tried again, and this time, to her own immense irritation, she heard a pleading note enter her voice. 'Tell him there are things I know, things he hasn't considered.'

One of the guards placed a heavy hand on her shoulder and Elena stiffened under it. 'Don't touch me.'

'For your own safety, Your Highness, you must return to the tent.' And, pushing her around, he forced her back into the tent as if she were a small child being marched to her room.

Khalil sat at the teakwood table in his private tent and with one lean finger traced the route through the desert from the campsite to Siyad. Three hundred miles. Three hundred miles to victory.

Reluctantly, yet unable to keep himself from it, he let his gaze flick to a corner of the map, an inhospitable area of bleak desert populated by a single nomadic tribe: his mother's people.

He knew Abdul-Hafiz was dead, and the people of his mother's tribe now supported him as the rightful ruler of Kadar. Yet though they'd even named him as Sheikh of their tribe, he hadn't been back yet to receive the honour.

He couldn't face returning to that barren bit of ground where he'd suffered for three long years.

His stomach still clenched when he looked at that corner of the map, and in his mind's eye he pictured Abdul-Hafiz's cruel face, his thin lips twisted into a mocking sneer as he raised the whip above Khalil's cringing form.

'The woman is asking for you.'

Khalil turned away from the map to see Assad standing in the doorway of his tent, the flaps drawn closed behind him.

'Queen Elena? Why?'

'She claims she has information.'

'What kind of information?'

Assad shrugged. 'Who knows? She is desperate, and most likely lying.'

Khalil drummed his fingers against the table. Elena was indeed desperate, and that made her reckless. Defiant. No doubt her bid to speak to him was some kind of ploy; perhaps she thought she could argue her way to freedom. It would be better, he knew, to ignore her request. Spend as little time as possible with the woman who was already proving to be an unwanted temptation.

'It is worth investigating,' he said after a moment. 'I'll see her.'

'Shall I summon her?'

'No, don't bother. I'll go to her tent.' Khalil rose from his chair, ignoring the anticipation that uncurled low in his belly at the thought of seeing Queen Elena again.

The wind whipped against him, stinging his face with grains of sand as he walked across the campsite to Elena's tent. Around him men hunkered down by fires or tended to their weapons or animals. At the sight of all this industry, all this loyalty, something both swelled and ached inside Khalil.

This was, he knew, the closest thing he'd had to family in twenty-nine years.

Dimah was family, of course, and he was incredibly thankful for what she'd done for him. She had, quite literally, saved him: provided for him, supported him, believed in him.

Yes, he owed Dimah a great deal. But she'd never understood what drove him, how much he needed to reclaim his inheritance, his very self. These men did.

Shaking off such thoughts, he strode towards Elena's tent, waving the guards aside as he drew back the flaps, only to come up short.

Elena was in the bath.

The intimacy of the moment struck him like a fist to the heart: the endless darkness outside, the candlelight flickering over the golden skin of her back, the only sound the slosh of the water against the sides of the deep copper tub as Elena washed herself—and then the hiss of his sudden, indrawn breath as a wave of lust crashed over him with the force of a tsunami.

She stiffened, the sponge dropping from her hand, and turned her head so their gazes met. Clashed. She didn't speak, didn't even move, and neither did Khalil. The moment spun out between them, a moment taut with expectation and yet beautiful in its simplicity.

She was beautiful, the elegant shape of her back reminding him of the sinuous curves of a cello. A single tendril of dark hair lay against the nape of her neck; the rest was piled on top of her head.

As if from a great distance Khalil registered her shuddering breath and knew she was frightened. Shame scorched him and he spun on his heel.

'I beg your pardon. I did not realise you were bathing. I'll wait outside.' He pushed outside the tent, the guards coming quickly to flank him, but he just shook his head and brushed them off. Lust still pulsed insistently inside him, an ache in his groin. He folded his arms across his chest and willed his body's traitorous reaction to recede.

Yet, no matter how hard he tried, he could not banish the image of Elena's golden perfection from his mind.

After a few endless minutes he heard a rustling behind him and Elena appeared, dressed in a white towelling robe that thankfully covered her from neck to toe.

'You may come in.' Her voice was husky, her cheeks flushed—although whether from the heat of the bath or their unexpected encounter he didn't know.

Khalil stepped inside the tent. Elena had already retreated to the far side, the copper tub between them like a barrier, her slight body swallowed up by the robe.

'I'm sorry,' Khalil said. 'I didn't know you were in the bath.'

'So you said.'

'You don't believe me?'

'Why should I believe anything you say?' she retorted. 'You haven't exactly been acting in an honourable fashion.'

Khalil drew himself up, any traces of desire evaporating in the face of her obvious scorn. 'And it would be honourable to allow my country to be ruled by a pretender?'

'A *pretender*?' She shook her head in derisive disbelief, causing a few more tendrils of hair to fall against her cheek. Khalil's hand twitched with the sudden, absurd urge to touch her, to brush those strands away from her face. He clenched his hand into a fist instead.

'Aziz is not the rightful heir to the throne.'

'I don't *care*!' she cried, her voice ringing out harsh and desperate. Khalil felt any soft longings in him harden, crystallise into determination. Of course she didn't care.

'I realise that, Your Highness,' he answered shortly. 'Although why you wish to marry Aziz is not clear to me. Power, perhaps.' He let her hear the contempt in his voice but she didn't respond to it, except to give one weary laugh.

'Power? I suppose you could say that.' She closed her eyes briefly, and when she opened them he was surprised to see so much bleak despair reflected in their grey-gold depths. 'All I meant was, none of it really matters to me, being here. I understand this—this conflict is very important to you. But keeping me here won't accomplish your goal.'

'You don't think so?'

'No.' Her mouth twisted in something like a smile. 'Aziz will just marry someone else. He still has four days.'

'I'm aware of the time that is left.' He regarded her thoughtfully, the bleakness still apparent in her eyes, the set of her shoulders and mouth both determined and courageous. He felt another flicker of admiration as well as a surge of curiosity. *Why* had she agreed to marry Aziz? What could such a marriage possibly give her?

'So why keep me here?' she pressed. 'If he can fulfil the terms of his father's will with another woman?'

'Because he won't.'

'But he will. We barely know each other. We've only met once before.'

'I know.'

'Then why do you think he would be loyal to me?' she asked and he felt a sudden flash of compassion as well as understanding, because he'd asked that question so many times himself. Why would anyone be loyal to him? Why should he trust anyone?

The person he'd loved most in the world had betrayed and rejected him utterly.

'To be frank,' he told her, 'I don't think loyalty is the issue. Politics are.'

'Exactly. So he'll just marry someone else.'

'And alienate his people even more? They love the idea of this wedding. They love it more than they do Aziz. And if he were to discard one woman for another...' *As our father did.* No, he had no wish to divulge that information to Elena just yet. He took a quick breath. 'It would not be popular. It would destabilise his rule even more.'

'But if he's going to lose his crown anyway...'

'But he won't, not necessarily. Did he not tell you?' Uncertainty flashed across her features and Khalil curved his mouth in a grim smile. 'The will states that, if Aziz does not marry within six weeks, he must call a national referendum. The people will then choose the new sheikh.'

She stared at him, her eyes widening. 'And you think that will be you?'

He let out a hard laugh. 'Don't sound so sceptical.'

'Who *are* you?'

'I told you, the next ruler of Kadar.' Her gaze moved over his face searchingly, and he saw despair creep back into her eyes.

'But Aziz could still go ahead and marry someone else while I'm stuck here in the desert. What happens then?'

'If he does that, it might lead to a civil war. I don't think he wishes for that to happen. Admittedly, Your Highness, I am taking a risk. You are right in saying that Aziz could marry someone else. But I don't think he will.'

'Why not just meet him and ask him to call the referendum?'

He shook his head. 'Because he knows he won't win it.'

'And if it comes to war? Are you prepared?'

'I will do what I must to secure my country's rule. Make no mistake about that, Queen Elena.' She flinched slightly at his implacable tone and something in Khalil softened just a little. None of this was Elena's fault. She was a casualty of a conflict that didn't involve her. In any other circumstance, he would have applauded her courage and determination.

'I'm sorry,' he said after a pause. 'I realise your plans to marry Aziz have been upset. But, considering how they were made so recently, I'm sure you'll recover.' He didn't mean to sound quite so cutting, but he knew he did, and he saw her flinch again.

She looked away, her gaze turning distant. 'You think so?' she said, not really a question, and again he heard the bleak despair and wondered at its source.

'I know so, Your Highness. I don't know why you decided to marry Aziz, but since it wasn't for love your heart is hardly broken.'

'And you know about broken hearts?' she answered with another weary laugh. 'You don't even seem to have one.'

'Perhaps I don't. But you didn't love him?' That *was* a question, of a sort. He was curious, even if he didn't want to be. He didn't want to know more about Elena, to wonder about her motives or her heart.

And yet still he asked.

'No,' she said after a moment. 'Of course I didn't—don't—love him. I barely know him. We met twice, for a couple of hours.' She shook her head, let out a long, defeated sigh, and then seemed to come to herself, straightening again, her eyes flashing once more. 'But I have your word you will release me after four days?'

'Yes. You have my word.' She relaxed slightly then, even as he stiffened. 'You don't think I'd hurt you?'

'Why shouldn't I? Kidnappers are usually capable of other crimes.'

'As I explained, this was a necessary evil, Your Highness, nothing more.'

'And what else will be a *necessary evil*, Khalil?' she answered back. He didn't like the hopelessness he saw in her eyes; it was as if the spark that had lit her from within had died out. He missed it. 'When you justify one thing, it becomes all too easy to justify another.'

'You sound as if you speak from experience.'

'I do.'

'Your own.'

A pause and her mouth firmed and tightened. 'Of sorts.'

He opened his mouth to ask another question, but then closed it abruptly. He didn't want to know. He didn't need to understand this woman; he simply needed her to stay put for a handful of days. He was sorry, more or less, for her disappointment. But that was all it was, a disappointment. An inconvenience, really. Her future, her very life, was not riding on a marriage to a stranger.

Not like his was.

'I promise I will not hurt you. And in four days you will be free.' She simply stared at him and, with one terse nod, he dismissed her, leaving the tent without another word.

CHAPTER THREE

ELENA WOKE SLOWLY, blinking in the bright sunlight that filtered through the small gap in the tent's flaps. Her body ached with tiredness; her mind had spun and seethed all night and she hadn't fallen asleep until some time near dawn.

Now she stretched and stared up at the rippling canvas of the tent, wondering what this day would bring.

She'd spent hours last night considering her options. She'd wondered if she could steal someone's mobile phone, make contact. Yet who would she call—the operator, to connect her to the Kadaran palace? Her Head of Council, who would probably be delighted by the news of her capture? In any case, she most likely couldn't get a signal out here.

Then she'd wondered if she could make a friend of one of the guards, get him to help her. That seemed even less likely; both of the guards she'd met had appeared utterly unmoved by her predicament.

Could she cause a fire, so its smoke might be caught by a satellite, a passing helicopter or plane?

Each possibility seemed more ludicrous than the last, and yet she refused to admit defeat. Giving in would mean losing her crown.

But the longer she stayed here, the more likely it was Aziz would marry someone else, no matter what Khalil said or thought. Or, even if he didn't, he wouldn't marry her. Maybe he would call this referendum and win the vote. He wouldn't need her at all.

But she still needed him, needed someone to marry her in the next month as she'd promised her Council, someone *she* was willing to marry, to father her children…

The thought caused her stomach to churn and her heart to sink. Her plan to marry Aziz had been desperate; finding another groom was outlandish. What was she going to *do*?

Sighing, she rose from the bed. A female voice sounded outside her tent, and a second later a woman entered, smiling and bearing a pitcher of fresh water.

'Good morning, Your Highness,' she said, ducking a quick curtsey, and Elena murmured back her own greeting, wondering if this woman might be the ally she was looking for.

The sight of the water in the woman's hands reminded her of her bath last night—and Khalil seeing her in it. Even now she felt her insides clench with a nameless emotion at the memory of his arrested look. The heat in his eyes had burned her with both pleasure and pain. To be desired, it was a fearsome thing—exciting, yes, but terrifying too, especially from a man like Khalil.

It had been foolish, she supposed, to take a bath, but when the two surly, silent guards had brought in the huge copper tub and filled it with steaming water, Elena had been unable to resist.

She'd been tired and sandy, every muscle aching with physical as well as emotional fatigue, and the thought of slipping into the rose-scented water, petals floating on top, had been incredibly appealing. A good wash would clear her head as well as clean her body and Khalil, she'd assumed, would not see her again that night.

And yet he'd seen her… Oh, how he'd seen her. She blushed to remember it, even though logically she knew he couldn't have seen much. The high sides of the tub would have kept her body from his sight, and in any case her back had been to him.

Even so she remembered the feel of his stilled gaze on her, the heat and intensity of it and, more alarmingly, her own answering response, everything inside her tightening and tautening, *waiting...*

'Is there anything else you need, Your Highness?' the woman asked, her voice pleasantly accented.

Yes, Elena thought, *my freedom*. She forced a smile. She needed this woman to be her friend. 'This is lovely, thank you. Were you the one who arranged the bath last night?'

The woman ducked her head. 'Yes, I thought you would like a wash.'

'It was wonderful, thank you.' Elena's mind raced. 'Where do you get the water? Is there an oasis here?'

'Yes, just beyond the rocks.'

'Is it very private? I'd love to have a swim some time, if I could.'

The woman smiled. 'If Sheikh Khalil approves, then I'm sure you could. It is lovely for swimming.'

'Thank you.' Elena didn't know if the oasis might provide her with an opportunity either to escape or attempt some kind of distraction to alert anyone who might be looking for her, but at least it was an option, a chance. Now she just had to get Khalil to agree to let her have a swim.

'When you are ready, you may break your fast outside,' the woman said. 'Sheikh Khalil is waiting.'

That was the second time the woman had called Khalil 'sheikh'. Was he a sheikh in his own right, Elena wondered, or did she already consider him as having the throne of Kadar? She wanted to ask Khalil just what made him feel so sure of his position, but she knew she wouldn't. She didn't want to know more about this man or, heaven forbid, find some sympathy for him. Her physical awareness of him was alarming enough.

A few minutes later, dressed in a pair of khakis and a

plain button-down shirt that had been provided for her, her hair neatly plaited, Elena stepped out of her tent.

The brilliance of the desert sun, the hard, bright blue of the sky and the perfect clarity of the air left her breathless for a moment. She was dazzled by the austere beauty of the desert, even though she didn't want to be. She didn't want to feel anything for any of it.

Khalil was eating by himself under an awning that had been set up above a raised wooden platform. He rose as she approached.

'Please. Sit.'

'Thank you.' She perched on the edge of a chair and Khalil arched an amused eyebrow.

'Courteous today, are we?'

Elena shrugged. 'I choose my battles.'

'I look forward to the next one.' He poured her coffee from an ornate brass pot; it looked thick and dark and smelled of cardamom. 'This is Kadaran coffee,' he told her. 'Have you ever tried it?'

She shook her head and took a tentative sip; the taste was strong but not unpleasant. Khalil nodded his approval. 'Would you have taken on Kadaran ways, if you'd become Aziz's bride?'

Elena stiffened. 'I could still become his bride, you know. He might find me.'

The look Khalil gave her was arrogant and utterly assured. 'I wouldn't get your hopes up, Your Highness.'

'Yours certainly seem high enough.'

He shrugged, one powerful shoulder lifting slightly, muscles rippling underneath the linen *thobe* he wore. 'As I told you before, the people of Kadar do not support Aziz.'

Surely he was exaggerating? Elena thought. Aziz had mentioned some instability, but not that he was an unpopular ruler. 'Outside of Siyad, you said,' she recalled. 'And why wouldn't they support him? He's the Sheikh's only son, and the succession has always been dynastic.'

Khalil's mouth tightened, his tawny eyes flashing fire before he shrugged again. 'Maybe you should take my advice and brush up on your Kadaran history.'

'And is there a book you suggest I read?' She raised her eyebrows, tried to moderate her tone. She was not doing herself any favours, arguing with him. 'Perhaps one I can take out of the library?' she added, in a poor attempt at levity.

Khalil's mouth twitched in a smile of what Elena suspected was genuine amusement. It lightened and softened him somehow, made him even more attractive than when he was cold and forbidding. 'I have a small library of books with me. I'll be happy to lend you one, although you won't find the answers you're looking for in a book.'

'Where will I find them, then?'

He hesitated and for a moment Elena thought he was going to say something else, something important. Then he shook his head. 'I don't think any answers would satisfy you, Your Highness, not right now. But when you're ready to listen, and consider there might be more to this story than what you've been told by Aziz, perhaps I'll enlighten you.'

'I should be so lucky,' she retorted, but for the first time since meeting Khalil she felt a flicker of real uncertainty. He was so *sure*. What if his claim had some legitimacy?

But, no, he was an insurgent. An impostor. He *had* to be. Anything else was unthinkable.

To her surprise Khalil leaned forward, placed his hand over hers. Elena stiffened under that small touch and it seemed as if the solid warmth of his hand spread throughout her whole body. 'You don't want to be curious,' he murmured. 'But you are.'

'Why should I be curious about a criminal?' she snapped, and he just smiled and removed his hand.

'Remember what I said. There is another side to the story.' He turned to go and Elena stared at him in frustration; she'd completely missed her opportunity to ask him about the oasis.

'And what am I meant to do for four days?' she called. 'Are you going to keep me imprisoned in my tent?'

'Only if you are foolish enough to attempt to escape.' Khalil turned to face her, his voice and face both hard once more.

'And if I did?'

'I would find you, hopefully before you were dead.'

'Charming.'

'The desert is a dangerous place. Regardless of the scorpions and snakes, a storm can arise in a matter of minutes and bury a tent, never mind a man, in seconds.'

'I know that.' She pressed her lips together and stared down at her plate; Khalil had served her some fresh fruit, dates, figs and succulent slices of melon. She picked up a fork and toyed with a bit of papaya.

'So I may trust you won't attempt an escape?' Khalil asked.

'Do you want me to promise?'

'No,' he answered after a moment. 'I don't trust promises. I just don't want your death on my conscience.'

'How thoughtful of you,' Elena answered sardonically. 'I'm touched.'

To her surprise he smiled again, revealing a surprising dimple in one cheek. 'I thought you would be.'

'So, if I'm not stupid enough to try and escape, may I go outside?' she asked. 'The woman who brought me water said there was an oasis here.' She held her breath, tried to keep her face bland.

'You mean Leila, Assad's wife. And, yes, you may go to the oasis if you like. Watch out for snakes.'

She nodded, her heart thumping with both victory and relief. She had a plan. She could finally *do* something.

'Are you going somewhere?' she asked, her gaze sliding to the horses that were being saddled nearby. If Khalil was gone, all the better.

'Yes.'

'Where?'

'To meet with some of the Bedouin tribes in this area of the desert.'

'Rallying support?' she queried, an edge to her voice, and he lifted his eyebrows.

'Remember what I said about arguing?'

'How was that arguing? I'm not going to just give up, if that's what you want. "Attack is the secret of defence",' she quoted recklessly. '"Defence is the planning of an attack".'

Khalil nodded, a slight smile on his lips. '*The Art of War* by Sun Tzu,' he said. 'Impressive.' She simply stared at him, chin jutted out, and he quoted back at her, '"He who knows when he can fight and when he cannot will be victorious".'

'Exactly.'

He laughed softly, shaking his head. 'So you think you can win in this situation, Your Highness, despite all I've said?'

'"The supreme art of war is to subdue the enemy without fighting".'

He cocked his head, his gaze sweeping over her almost lazily. 'And how do you intend to subdue me?'

Surely he hadn't meant those words to have a sensual intent, a sexual innuendo, yet somehow they had. Elena felt it in the warmth that stole through her body, turning her bones liquid and her mind to mush.

Khalil held her gaze, his eyes glowing gold and she simply stared back, unable to reply or even think. Finally her brain sputtered back into gear and she forced out, '"Let your plans be dark and impenetrable as night".'

'Clearly you've studied him well. It makes me curious, since your country has been at peace for nearly a thousand years.'

'There are different kinds of wars.' And the war she fought was scarily subtle: a murmured word, a whispered rumour. She was constantly on the alert for an attack.

'So there are. And I pray, Your Highness, that this war for the throne of Kadar might be fought without a single drop of blood being spilled.'

'You don't think Aziz will fight you?'

'I hope he knows better. Now, enough. I must ride. I hope you enjoy your day.'

With that he strode towards the horses, his body dark and powerful against the brilliant blue sky, the blazing sun. When he had gone Elena felt, absurdly, as if something was missing that she'd both wanted and enjoyed.

After Khalil had left, riding off into the desert with several of his men, great clouds of dust and sand billowing behind them, Elena went back to her tent. To her surprise, she saw a book—*The Making of Modern Kadar*—had been placed on her bedside table. Was Khalil being thoughtful, she wondered, or mocking?

Curious, she flipped through the book. She already knew the basics of Kadar's history: its many years of peace, isolated as it was on a remote peninsula, jutting out into the Arabian Sea. While war had passed it by, so had technology, and for centuries it had remained as it had always been, a cluster of tribal communities with little interest beyond their nomadic life of shepherding. Then, in the early 1800s, Sheikh Ahmad al Bakir, the great-great-grandfather of Hashem, had united the tribes and created a monarchy. He'd ruled Kadar for nearly fifty years, and since then there had only been peace and prosperity.

None of it told her why Khalil believed he was the rightful ruler and not Aziz, Hashem's only son. The book didn't even hint at any insurgency or civil unrest; if it was to be believed, nothing had caused so much as a flicker of unease in the peaceful, prosperous rule of the House of al Bakir.

She tossed the book aside, determined not to wonder any more about Khalil. She didn't need to know whether his claim had any merit. She wasn't going to care.

She just wanted to get out of here, however she could. Resolutely, she went in search of Leila. The guards outside her tent summoned her, and Leila was happy to show her the way to the oasis. She even brought Elena a swimming costume and a packed lunch. It was all so civilised, Elena almost felt guilty at her deception.

Almost.

Alone in her tent, she searched for what she needed. The legs of the table were too thick, but the chairs might do.

Kneeling on the floor of the tent, the sound muffled by a pillow, she managed to snap several slats from the back of a chair. She stuffed the slats in the bag with the picnic and with her head held high walked out of the tent.

The guards let her pass and Leila directed her down a worn path that wound between two towering boulders.

'"Threading the needle", it's called,' Leila said, for the path between the rocks was incredibly narrow. 'It is a beautiful spot. See for yourself.'

'And you're not worried I'll make a run for it?' Elena asked, trying to keep her voice light. Leila's face softened in sympathy, causing another flash of guilt that she ruthlessly pushed away. These people were her captors, no matter how kind Leila was being. And she *had* to escape somehow.

'I know this is difficult for you, Your Highness, but the Sheikh is a good man. He is protecting you from an unhappy marriage, whether you realise it or not.'

Now *that* was putting quite a spin on things. 'I wasn't aware that Khalil was concerned with the happiness of my marriage,' Elena answered. 'Only with being Sheikh.'

'He is Sheikh already, of one of the desert tribes,' Leila answered. 'And he is the rightful heir to the throne of

Kadar. A great injustice was done to him, and it is finally time to make it right.'

Again Elena felt that uncomfortable flicker of uncertainty. Leila sounded so sure…as sure as Khalil. 'What injustice?' she asked before she could think better of it. Leila shook her head.

'It is not for me to say. But if you had married Aziz, Your Highness, you would have been marrying an impostor. Very few people outside of Siyad believe Aziz should be Sheikh.'

It was what Khalil had said, yet Elena could not accept it. 'But *why*?'

Leila's forehead creased in a troubled frown. 'You must ask Sheikh Khalil—'

'He's not really Sheikh,' Elena interjected, unable to keep herself from it. 'Not of Kadar. Not yet.'

'But he should be,' Leila said quietly, and to Elena she sounded utterly certain. 'Ask him,' the older woman advised. 'He will tell you the truth.'

But did she want to know the truth? Elena wondered as she walked between the towering rocks towards the oasis. If Khalil had a legitimate claim to the throne, what did it mean for her—and her marriage?

Would she still marry Aziz if he wasn't the rightful Sheikh? Would her Council even want her to? The point, Elena reminded herself, was most likely moot—unless she got out of here.

After walking between the boulders she emerged onto a flat rock overlooking a small, shimmering pool shaded by palm trees. The sun sparkled on the water as if on a metal plate, the sky brilliant blue above. The air was hot, dry and still, perfect for a swim.

She glanced around, wondering if the guards had followed her, but she could see no one. Just in case, she made a show of putting down her bag, spreading her towel on the rock. She slathered herself with sunscreen before she stripped down to the plain black swimming costume Leila had provided.

She glanced around again; she was definitely alone. No one had followed her from the camp.

And why should anyone? She was but a five-minute walk from her tent, in the middle of the desert, the middle of nowhere. In every direction the desert stretched, endless sand and towering black rocks, both bleak and beautiful.

There was, Elena knew, nowhere to go, nothing to do but wait and hope that Aziz found her.

Or send a signal.

She reached for her bag and took out the slats she'd broken from the chair. A few weedy-looking plants grew by the oasis's edge, and she took them and made a small, rather pathetic-looking pile. She wasn't going to get much of a blaze from this, Elena realised disconsolately, but it would have to do. It was her only chance. If someone saw the smoke from her fire, they might investigate, might look for her.

Resolutely, she started rubbing the sticks together.

Fifteen minutes later she had blisters on both hands and the sticks were a little warm. She hadn't seen so much as a spark. Frustrated, she laid the sticks aside and rose from the rock. The air was hot and still and the shimmering waters of the oasis looked extremely inviting.

Balancing on her tiptoes, she executed a neat dive into the pool. The water closed around her, cool and refreshing, and she swam under water for a few metres before she surfaced, treading water, not knowing what was on the bottom and not particularly wishing to touch it with her bare feet.

Even if she managed to start a fire, she thought, what would distinguish it from any other camp fire? She'd have to get a really big blaze going for someone to take notice. She'd have to set the whole camp on fire.

Her plan, Elena realised, was ridiculous. The sense of purpose that had buoyed her all morning left her in a depressing rush. Yet even so she decided to try again. It wasn't as if she had many, or any, other options.

She swam to the side of the oasis and hauled herself, dripping, onto the rock ledge. Drying herself off, she knelt before the sticks again and started to rub.

Five minutes later she saw the first tiny spark kindle between the sticks. Hope leapt in her chest and she rubbed harder; some of the dried plants and leaves she'd gathered caught the spark and the first small flame flickered. She let out a cry of triumph.

'Don't move.'

Everything in Elena stilled at the sound of that low, deadly voice. She looked up, her heart lurching against her ribs at the sight of Khalil standing just a few feet away. His eyes were narrowed, his mouth thinned, everything about him tense and still.

Her heart started to pound and then it seemed to stop completely as Khalil slowly, steadily, raised the pistol he'd been holding and pointed it straight at her.

CHAPTER FOUR

THE SOUND OF the pistol firing echoed through the still air, bounced off the boulders and rippled the still waters of the oasis.

Dispassionately Khalil watched as the snake leapt and twisted in the air before falling a few feet away, dead.

He turned back to look at Elena and swore softly when he saw her sway, her face drained of colour, her pupils dilated with terror. Without even considering what he was doing, or why, he strode forward, caught her in his arms and drew her shuddering body to his chest.

'I killed it, Elena,' he said as he stroked her dark hair. 'It's dead. You don't need to be afraid now.'

She pushed away from him, her whole body still trembling. 'What's dead?'

Khalil stared at her for several seconds as the meaning of her question penetrated. He swore again. 'I shot the snake! Did you not see it, but three feet from you, and ready to strike?'

She just stared at him with wide, blank eyes, and forcibly he took her jaw in his hand and turned her head so she could see the dead viper. She blanched, drawing her breath in a ragged gasp.

'I thought...'

'You thought I was aiming at you?' Khalil finished flatly. His stomach churned with a sour mix of guilt and anger. 'How could you think such a thing?' He didn't wait for her answer, for he knew what it would be: *because you kidnapped me*. 'I promised you I wouldn't hurt you.'

'And you also said you didn't trust anyone's promises. Neither do I, Khalil.' She tried to move away from him but she stumbled, her body still shaking, and Khalil pulled her towards him once more. 'Don't—'

'You've had a shock.' He sat down on the rock, drawing her onto his lap. It was a jolt to his system, to feel a warm body against his, yet it also felt far too good, familiar in a way that made no sense, yet felt intrinsically *right*.

He felt the stiffness in her body, saw the way she angled her face away from him and knew that just as he was she was trying to keep herself apart, stand on pride. He saw so much of himself in her and it unnerved him. It touched him in a way he didn't expect or even understand. From the moment he'd met Elena she'd *done* things to him. Not just to his body, but to his heart.

Gently he stroked her damp hair away from her face. She let out a shuddering breath and relaxed against him, her cheek against his chest. Something deep and fierce inside Khalil, some part of him he hadn't thought still existed, let out a roar of both satisfaction and need.

He tucked a tendril behind her ear just as he'd wanted to yesterday. Her eyes were closed, her dark lashes sweeping her pale cheeks.

'You pointed that gun at me,' she whispered, her voice sounding distant and numb.

'I pointed it at the *snake*,' Khalil answered. He knew she was in shock, trying to process what had happened, but he still felt a flash of anger, a stirring of guilt. He should have made her feel safer. She should have been able to trust him.

This, when you trust no one?

'A black snake,' he continued, keeping his voice steady and calm. 'They can be deadly.'

'I didn't even see it.' He thought she was recovering

from the shock but then she let out a little shuddering sob and pressed her face against his chest.

His whole body jolted with the fierce pleasure of having her curl into him, seek his comfort. When had anyone ever done that? When had anyone wanted something real and tender from him? And when had he felt it in response, this yearning and protectiveness?

He could not remember a time, and it forced him to acknowledge the stark emptiness of his life, the years of relentless and ruthless striving, utterly without comfort.

'There, there, *habiibii*. You're safe now. Safe.' The words were strange to him, yet he spoke them without thinking, stroking her hair, his arms tight around her. He could feel her shoulders shake and he could tell from her ragged breathing she was doing her best to keep herself from crying. His throat tightened with emotion he hadn't felt in decades.

After a moment she pushed away from him, her eyes still dry, her face pale but resolutely composed.

'I'm sorry. You must think I'm being ridiculous.' She sat stiffly in his lap now, her chin lifted at a queenly angle. Already Khalil missed the feel of her against him.

'Not at all,' he answered. He suppressed the clamour of his own feelings, forced it all back down again. 'I realise that a great deal has happened to you in a short amount of time.' He hesitated, choosing his words with care, wanting and even needing her to understand. To believe him. 'I'm sorry for the fear and unhappiness I have caused you.'

For a second, no more, he thought she did. Her face softened, her lips parting, and then she gave a little shake of her head and scrambled off his lap. 'Even though it was entirely preventable?'

Their moment of startling intimacy was over and Khalil, half-amazed at his own reaction, felt a sudden piercing of grief at its loss.

* * *

Elena stood on the rock, trying to calm her thundering heart—and ignore the ache Khalil's touch had created in her. She couldn't remember the last time she'd been held so tenderly, spoken to so gently.

He's your captor, she reminded herself grimly. *He kidnapped you.* But in that moment he'd been incredibly kind, and her body and heart had responded to it like a flower unfurling in the sunlight.

When had someone comforted her, touched her, understood her? She'd lived such a solitary existence, first as an only child, then as an orphan queen. The one person she'd let close had betrayed her utterly.

Just as Khalil will betray you. At least he was honest about his intentions.

Khalil gazed at her, his expression inscrutable, any remnant of tenderness erased completely from his harsh features. He glanced at her pathetic pile of plants and broken chair slats; the tiny flame she'd been kindling had gone out. 'What on earth were you doing?' he asked. He turned back to her, his mouth twisting with bemusement. 'Were you building a *fire*?' She didn't answer and his mouth curved into a smile as he shook his head. She almost thought she heard admiration in his voice. 'You were building a signal fire, weren't you?'

Elena lifted her chin. 'And if I was?'

'It's the most pathetic signal fire I've ever seen.' Khalil smiled, inviting her to share the joke, his teasing gentle, compassion kindling in his eyes—a compassion she hadn't seen before and hadn't thought he possessed.

Elena felt an answering smile tug at her own mouth. It *was* pathetic. And it felt good to joke, to laugh, even with Khalil. Especially with Khalil. 'I know. I realised it wasn't going to work. It would be far too small if it had even caught at all. But I had to do something.'

Khalil nodded, his expression serious once more. 'I understand that, Elena,' he said quietly. 'You know, we are a lot alike. We both fight against what we cannot change.'

'It looks to me like you're trying to change something,' she retorted, and he inclined his head in acknowledgement.

'Yes, now. But there was a time when I couldn't. When I was powerless and angry but determined to keep fighting, because at least it reminded me I was alive. That I had something to fight for.'

And, God help her, she knew how that felt. The last four years, she'd felt that every day. 'If you know what that feels like,' she asked in a raw voice, 'then how can you keep me prisoner?'

For a second, no more, Khalil looked conflicted. Torn. Then his eyes veiled and his mouth firmed, everything about him hardening. 'We are not as alike as all that,' he said shortly. 'You might be a prisoner, Elena, but you are treated with respect and courtesy. You have every comfort available.'

'Does that really matter—?'

'Trust me,' he cut her off, his voice cold now, implacable. 'It matters.'

'When have you felt like a prisoner?'

He stared at her for a long moment then gave a little shake of his head. 'We should return to the camp.'

She still wanted answers, even if she shouldn't ask the questions, shouldn't get to know this man any more. Yet she did, because he understood her in a way no one else did. She wanted, she realised, to understand him. 'Why did you come looking for me?'

'I was worried about you.'

'That I'd escape?'

A tiny smile lightened his features. 'No, I'm afraid not. I was worried you might encounter a snake, and I was very nearly right. They like to sun themselves on these rocks.'

'You did warn me.'

'Even so.'

She shook her head, her throat suddenly tight because everything about this was so strange. Khalil was her captor. Her enemy. But he'd also treated her with more gentleness than any other human being that she could remember, and if he had a legitimate claim to the throne...

'What is it, Elena?' he asked quietly.

'I don't know what to think,' she admitted. 'I don't even know if I want to ask you.'

'Ask me what?'

She took a breath, let it out slowly. 'Your side of the story.'

Something flared in his eyes, something she couldn't name, but it had her body responding, heat unfurling low in her belly. Then it died out and his expression hardened once more. 'You don't want to change your mind.'

'You don't know what this marriage means for me, Khalil.'

'Then why don't you tell me?'

'What good would it do? Would you lose the chance of your crown so I can keep mine?'

He raised his eyebrows, his expression still uncompromising. 'Are you in danger of losing it?'

She didn't answer, because she'd already said too much and the last thing she wanted to do was admit to Khalil how shaky her throne really was. So far she'd managed to hide the threat Markos posed to her. If it became public, she knew it would just give him power. She could already imagine the newspaper headlines about the teenaged queen and the stupid mistake she'd made, trusting someone, thinking he loved her.

She wouldn't do that again.

And certainly not with Khalil.

Yet even so part of her yearned to tell him the truth, to unburden herself, have someone understand, sympathise and even offer advice.

Like Paulo had?

Why on earth was she thinking of trusting Khalil when she knew to trust no one? What about this man made her want to break her own rules?

Because he understands you.

'Like you said, we should return to the camp,' she said and with her head held high she walked past him, back through the boulders.

As soon as she got back to her tent, Elena stripped off her swimming costume and dressed in the clothes she'd been given that morning. She felt more trapped now than she had since Khalil had first forced her into the car, but the prison this time was one of her own making. Her own mind. Her own heart.

She knew it was the coward's way not to listen to Khalil, not to ask what his side of the story was. Would she really want to marry Aziz if he wasn't the rightful Sheikh?

And yet he had to be, she told herself as she sat down on the bed. *He had to be.*

Because if he wasn't…

It didn't even matter, she reminded herself with a gusty sigh, dropping her head into her hands. She wasn't going to marry Aziz. No matter how gentle and tender he'd been with her today, Khalil still intended keeping her until the six weeks were up. Soon Aziz would have no reason to marry her.

Whether she wanted to or not.

She looked up, her gaze unfocused as she recalled the way Khalil had held her; the soft words he had spoken; the way he'd stroked her hair; the thud of his heart against her cheek.

She felt deep in her bones that he'd been sincere, and the realisation both terrified and thrilled her. She didn't have real relationships. She didn't know how. She'd been shy as a child, her parents distant figures, her only company a nanny and then a governess. Even if she'd wanted, yearned, for such things, she hadn't known how to go about getting them—and then Paulo had broken her trust and destroyed her faith in other people and, even worse, her faith in herself and her own judgement.

Was she misjudging Khalil now? Was it simply her pathetic inexperience with men and life that made her crave more of that moment, more tenderness, more contact?

Nothing about their relationship, if she could even use that word, was real.

Yet it *felt* real. She felt as if Khalil understood and even liked her for who she was. Maybe that was just wishful thinking, but whatever her association with Khalil was she knew she needed to know the truth. To ask for his side of the story…and face the consequences of whatever he told her.

She let out a shuddering breath, the decision made.

A little while later Leila slipped into the tent, smiling and curtseying as she caught sight of Elena. 'I've brought fresh clothes and water for washing. Sheikh Khalil has invited you to dine with him tonight.'

'He has?' Surprise, and a damning pleasure, rippled through her. 'Why?'

Leila's smile widened. 'Why shouldn't he, Your Highness?'

Why should he?

His reasons didn't matter, she told herself. This could be her opportunity to ask Khalil about his claim to the throne. And if she felt a little flare of anticipation at seeing him, at spending time with him, then so be it.

'Look at the dress he has brought you,' Leila said and, opening a box, she withdrew a dress of silvery grey from folds of tissue paper.

It was both beautiful and modest, the material as delicate and silky as a spider's web. Elena touched it before she could stop herself.

'I'm not sure why I need to wear that,' she said sharply,

drawing her hand away as if the fragile material had burned her. The temptation to try it on, to feel feminine and beautiful, was overwhelming.

Leila's face fell and she laid the dress down on the bed. 'You would look beautiful in it, Your Highness.'

'I don't need to look beautiful. I'm being held captive in a desert camp.' *And she needed to remember that. To stay strong.*

She turned away abruptly, hating that she sounded petulant and childish, and hating even more that she was tempted to wear the dress and have dinner with Khalil.

Hear his side of the story.

Quietly Leila folded the dress and returned it to the box. Elena felt even worse. 'Shall I tell Sheikh Khalil you wish to remain in your tent tonight?'

Conflicted, Elena turned back to Leila. 'I don't—' She stopped, took a breath. She was being a coward, hiding in her tent. She needed to face her fears. Face Khalil. If she learned just what his side of the story was, she'd be able to make a more informed decision about her own future. She'd know all the facts. Know her enemy.

Even if he didn't feel like her enemy any more.

'You may tell Khalil I'll eat with him,' Elena said. 'Thank you, Leila.' She glanced down at the dress, an ache of longing rising in her. It was such a lovely gown. 'And you may leave the dress.'

An hour later Leila escorted Elena to Khalil's private tent. Her heart started thudding and her palms felt damp as she stepped inside the luxurious quarters.

She felt self-conscious in the dress Leila had brought, as if she were dressing up for a date, but she also enjoyed the feel of the silky fabric against her skin, the way it swirled around her ankles as she moved. And, a tiny, treacherous voice whispered, she liked the thought of Khalil seeing her in it.

Everything in her rebelled at the realisation. She shouldn't want to please Khalil. She *couldn't* start to feel something for him. It would be beyond stupid—it would be dangerous.

As she came into the tent, she saw candlelight flickering over the low table that had been set with a variety of dishes. Silk and satin pillows were scattered around it in the Arabic style of dining, rather than sitting in chairs as she was used to.

Khalil emerged from the shadows, dressed in a loose, white cotton shirt and dark trousers; he'd taken off the traditional *thobe* she'd seen him in before. With his golden eyes and midnight hair, his chiselled jaw glinting with dark stubble, he looked like a sexy and dangerous pirate. Dangerous, she told herself, being the operative word.

Elena swallowed audibly as Khalil's heated gaze swept over her. 'You look lovely, Your Highness.'

'I'm not sure what the point of this dress is,' Elena retorted. 'Or this meal.' She was feeling far too vulnerable already, and attack was her best defence. She'd learned that in the Council Room; it had helped keep the crown on her head for four years.

When Markos had mocked her plans for better childcare provision, saying how women didn't need to work, Elena had come back with the percentages of women who did. When he'd belittled her idea for an arts festival, she'd pointed out the increased tourist revenues such events would bring. She'd refused to back down, and it was probably why he hated her. Why he wanted to end her rule.

Khalil had been walking towards her with graceful, predatory intent, but he stopped at her sharp words and raised an eyebrow. 'You complained this morning about being kept in your tent like a prisoner. I thought you would enjoy having company, even if it is mine.' A smile flickered over his face and died. 'Likewise, I thought you might prefer a dress to the admittedly more suitable khakis. I'm sorry if I was wrong.'

Now she felt ridiculous and even a little ashamed, almost

as if she'd hurt his feelings. Khalil waited, his expression ironed out to blandness. 'This is all very civilised,' Elena finally managed.

'It's meant to be civilised, Elena,' he answered. 'I have told you before, I am neither a terrorist nor a thug. Your stay here is, I'm afraid, a necessary—'

'Evil,' she filled in before she could help herself.

'Measure,' Khalil answered. Suddenly and surprisingly, he looked weary. 'If you are going to fight me all evening, perhaps you would prefer to eat in your tent. Or will you try to set fire to this one?'

Elena knew then that she didn't want to fight any more. What was the point? Khalil wasn't going to let her go. And she was wearing a beautiful dress, about to eat a lovely meal with a very attractive man. Maybe she should just enjoy herself. It was a novel concept; so much of her life as queen, and even before she'd ascended the throne, had been about duty. Sacrifice. When had anything been about pleasure?

She gave him a small smile and glanced consideringly at the creamy candles in their bronze holders. 'That would make a big enough signal fire.'

Khalil chuckled softly. 'Don't even think of it, Elena.'

'I wasn't,' she admitted. 'I've come to realise that setting a fire won't do me much good.'

'You have another idea?' he asked and walked forward to take her hand, the slide of his fingers across hers shooting sparks all the way up to her elbow.

'Well, I was thinking of trying to charm you into letting me go,' Elena answered lightly. She did a little twirl in her dress. 'The dress might help.'

Khalil's eyes gleamed. 'You'd tempt a saint, but I'm afraid I'm made of sterner stuff. Flirting won't get you very far.'

She drew back, a blush scorching her cheeks. 'I wasn't *flirting.*'

'No?' Khalil arched his eyebrows as he drew her down to the table. 'Pity.'

Even more disconcerted by his response, Elena fussed with positioning herself on the silken pillows, arranging the folds of her dress around her. Khalil sat opposite her, reclining on one elbow, every inch the relaxed and confident sheikh.

Sheikh. Yes, lying on the pillows, the candlelight glinting on his dark hair, he looked every inch the sheikh.

'Let me serve you,' Khalil said, and lifted the lids on several silver chafing dishes. He ladled some lamb stewed in fragrant spices onto her plate, along with couscous mixed with vegetables.

'It smells delicious,' Elena murmured. 'Thank you.' Khalil raised an eyebrow.

'So polite,' he said with a soft laugh. 'I'm waiting for the sting.'

'I'm hungry,' she answered, which was no answer at all because she didn't know what she was doing. What she felt.

'Then you must eat up,' Khalil said lightly. 'You are too thin, at least by Kadaran standards.'

She *was* thin, mainly because constant stress and anxiety kept her from eating properly. 'And you are familiar with Kadaran standards?' she asked. 'You said something about living in America before, didn't you?'

'I spent my adolescence in the United States,' he answered, his tone rather flat. He handed her a platter of bread, his expression shuttered, and Elena felt a surge of curiosity about this man and his experience.

'Is that why your English is so good?'

A smile flickered across his face, banishing the frown that had settled between his brows when she'd asked about where he had lived. 'Thank you. And, yes, I suppose it is.'

Elena sat back, taking dainty bites of the delicious lamb. 'How long have you been back in Kadar?'

'Six months. Is this an inquisition, Elena?' That smile now deepened, revealing the dimple Elena had seen before. '"Know your enemies and know yourself, and you can win a hundred battles".'

'You are quite familiar with *The Art of War*.'

'As are you,' he observed.

'How come you know it so well?'

'Because my life has been one of preparing for battle.'

'To become Sheikh of Kadar.'

'Yes.'

'But you're already a sheikh, aren't you? Leila told me...'

He shrugged. 'Of a small tribe in the northern desert. My mother's people.'

He was silent and so was she, the only sounds the wind ruffling the sides of the tent, the gentle clink of their dishes. Elena gazed at him, the harsh planes of his face, the sculpted fullness of his lips. Hard and soft, a mass of contradictions, this gentle kidnapper of hers. Her stomach twisted. What was she *doing*? How stupid was she being, to actually consider believing this man, trusting him?

She could tell herself she was here because she needed to know her enemy, needed to make an informed decision about her future, but Elena knew she was fooling herself. She was here because she wanted to be here. And she wanted to trust Khalil because she liked him. As a person. As a man.

'I want to hear the other side of the story,' she said quietly, and Khalil glanced up at her, his expression watchful, even wary.

'Do you,' he said, not a question, and she nodded and swallowed.

'Everyone around you is so sure, Khalil, of your right to the throne. I don't think they're brainwashed or deluded, so...' She spread her hands, tried for a smile. 'There must be some reason why people think you are the rightful sheikh. Tell me what it is.'

* * *

Tell me what it is. A simple request, yet one that felt like peeling back his skin, exposing his heart. Admitting his shame.

Khalil glanced away from Elena, his gaze distant, unfocused. He'd said before he'd tell her his side of the story when she was ready to listen, and here she was—ready.

The trouble was, he wasn't.

'Khalil,' Elena said softly. His name sounded right on her lips in a way that made everything in Khalil both want and rebel.

What was he doing? How had he got to this place, with this woman? It had started, perhaps, from the first moment he'd laid eyes on her. When, in what could be considered courage or folly or both, she'd attempted to escape. When he'd seen both fear and pride in her eyes and known exactly how she'd felt.

When he'd held her in his arms and she'd curled into him, seeking the solace that he'd freely, gladly, given.

And now she wanted more. Now she wanted the truth, which he'd told her he would tell her, except now that she'd actually asked he felt wary, reluctant. *Afraid.*

What if she didn't believe him? *What if she did?*

Finally Khalil spoke. 'My mother,' he said slowly, 'was Sheikh Hashem's first wife.'

Elena's eyes widened, although with disbelief, confusion or simply surprise he couldn't tell. 'What—who was your father?'

He bared his teeth in a smile that was a sign of his pain rather than any humour or happiness. 'Sheikh Hashem, of course.'

A hand flew to her throat. 'You mean you are Aziz's *brother*?'

'Half-brother, to be precise. Older half-brother.'

'But…' She shook her head, and now she definitely seemed disbelieving. Khalil felt something that had started to unfurl inside him begin to wither. *Good.* It was better this way. She wouldn't believe him, and he wouldn't care. It would be easy then. Painful, but easy. 'How can that be?' she asked. 'There's no mention of you anywhere, not even in that book!'

He laughed, the sound hard and bitter, revealing. 'So you read the book?'

'A bit.'

'There wouldn't be a mention of me in it. My father did his best to erase my existence from the world. But the Bedouin tribes, my mother's people, they have not forgotten me.' He hated how defensive he sounded. As if he needed to prove himself, as if he wanted her to believe him.

She didn't matter. Her opinion didn't matter. Why had he even asked her to dinner? Why had he given her that dress?

Because you wanted to please her. Because you wanted to see her again, touch her again...

Fool.

'Why would your father wish to erase your existence, Khalil?'

He gave her a glittering, challenging stare. 'Do you know who Aziz's mother is?'

Elena shrugged. 'Hashem's wife. Her name, I believe, is Hamidyah. She died a few years ago, Aziz told me.'

'Yes, she did. And, before she was my father's second wife, she was his mistress. She bore him a bastard, and my father claimed him as one. Aziz.' He let out a slow breath, one hand clenching involuntarily against his thigh. 'Then my father tired of my mother, his first wife, but Kadaran law has always dictated that the reigning monarch take only one wife.' He gave her the semblance of a smile. 'Not a moral stance, mind you, simply a pragmatic one: fewer contenders for the throne. I suspect it's why Kadar has enjoyed so many years of peace.'

'So you're saying he got rid of his wife? And—and of you? So he could marry Hamidyah?' Elena was gazing at him with an emotion he couldn't decipher. Was it confusion, disbelief or, God help him, pity? Did she think he was deluded?

'You don't believe me,' Khalil stated flatly. His stomach felt like a stone. He wasn't angry with her, he realised with a flash of fury he could only direct at himself; he was hurt.

'It seems incredible,' Elena said slowly. 'Surely someone would have known...?'

'The desert tribes know.'

'Does Aziz?'

'Of course he does.' The words came fast, spiked with bitterness. 'We met, you know, as boys.' Just weeks before he'd been torn from his family. 'Never since, although I've seen his photograph in the gossip magazines.'

Elena shook her head slowly. 'But if he knows you are the rightful heir...'

'Ah, but you see, my father is cleverer than that. He charged my mother with adultery and claimed I was not his son. He banished me from the palace when I was seven years old.'

Elena gaped at him. *'Banished...'*

'My mother as well, to a remote royal residence where she lived in isolation. She died just a few months later, although I didn't know that for many years. From the day my father threw me from the palace, I never saw her again.' He spoke dispassionately, even coldly, because if he didn't he was afraid of how he might sound. What he might reveal. Already he felt a tightness in his throat and he took a sip of wine to ease it.

'But that's terrible,' Elena whispered. She looked stricken, but her response didn't gratify Khalil. He felt too exposed for that.

'It's all ancient history,' he dismissed. 'It hardly matters now.'

'Doesn't it? This is why you're seeking the throne, as—'

'As revenge?' He filled in. 'No, Elena, it's not for revenge. It's because it's my *right*.' His voice throbbed with conviction. 'I am my father's first-born. When he set my mother aside he created deep divisions in a country that has only known peace. If you've wondered why Aziz does not have the support of his whole country, it's because too many people know he is not the rightful heir. He is popular in Siyad because he is cosmopolitan and charming, but the heart of this country is not his. It is mine.' He stared at her, his chest heaving, willing her to believe him. Needing her to.

'How can you be sure,' she whispered, 'that your mother didn't have an affair?'

'Of course I'm sure.' He heard his voice, as sharp as a blade. Disappointment dug deep. No, a feeling worse than disappointment, weaker—this damnable hurt. He took a steadying breath. 'My mother knew the consequences of an affair: banishment, shame, a life cut off from everyone and everything she knew. It would not have been worth the risk.'

'But you would have just been a boy. How could you have known?'

'I knew everyone around her believed her to be innocent. I knew her serving maids cried out at the injustice of it. I knew no man ever stepped forward to claim her or me, and my father couldn't even name the man who'd allegedly sired me. My father's entire basis for banishing both my mother and me was the colour of my eyes.'

Elena stared at him, her own golden-grey eyes filled with not confusion or disbelief but with something that was nearly his undoing: *compassion*.

'Oh, Khalil,' she whispered.

He glanced away, afraid of revealing himself. His jaw worked but he could not form words. Finally he choked out, 'People protested at the time. They said there wasn't enough proof. But then my mother died before he actually married Hamidyah, so it was, in the end, all above board.'

'And what about you?'

He couldn't admit what had happened to him: those years in the desert, the awful shame, even though part of him wanted to, part of him wanted to bare himself to this woman, give her his secrets. To trust another person, and with more than he ever had before, even as a child. He suppressed that foolish impulse and lifted one shoulder in what he hoped passed as an indifferent shrug. 'I was raised by my mother's sister, Dimah, in America. I never saw my father again.'

'And the people accepted it all?' she said quietly, only half a question. 'Aziz as the heir, even though they must have remembered you…'

'My father was a dictator. No one possessed the courage to question his actions while he was alive.'

'Why did Sheikh Hashem make such a strange will?' Elena burst out. 'Commanding Aziz to marry?'

'I think he was torn. Perhaps he realised the mistake he'd made in banishing me, but did not want to admit it. He was a proud man.' Khalil shrugged again. 'Forcing Aziz to marry would make him commit to Kadar and give up his European ways. But calling a national referendum if he didn't…' Khalil smiled grimly. 'My father must have known it was a chance for me to become Sheikh. Maybe that is just wishful thinking on my part, but I'd like to think he regretted, even if just in part, what he did to my mother and me.'

'And do you think people would accept you, if you did become Sheikh?'

'Some might have difficulty but, in time, yes. I believe they would.'

He stared at her then, willing her to tell him she believed him. Wanting, even needing, to hear it.

She looked away. Khalil's insides clenched with a helpless, hopeless anger.

Then she turned back to him, her eyes as wide and clear as twin lakes. 'Then we really are alike,' she said quietly. 'For we are both fighting for our crowns.'

CHAPTER FIVE

KHALIL'S GAZE HAD blazed anger but Elena saw something beneath the fury: *grief*. A grief she understood and felt herself. And, even though she didn't want to, she felt a sympathy for Khalil, a compassion and even an anger on his behalf. He'd been terribly wronged, just as Leila had said.

She thought of him as a boy, being banished from his family and home. She imagined his confusion and fear, the utter heartbreak of losing everything he'd known and held dear.

Just as she had.

She'd been a bit older, but her family had been wrenched from her in a matter of moments, just as Khalil's had. She was fighting to keep her rightful title, just as Khalil was.

With a jolt she realised what this meant: she believed him. She believed he was the rightful heir.

For a second everything in her rebelled. *You believed before. You trusted before. And this man has kidnapped you—how can you be so stupid?*

Yet she'd heard the sincerity in Khalil's voice. She'd felt his pain. She knew him in a way she hadn't known anyone else, because they were so alike.

She believed him.

'How are you fighting for your crown, Elena?' he asked quietly.

She hesitated, because honesty didn't come easily, and letting herself be vulnerable felt akin to pulling out her fingernails one by one. She'd hardened her heart in the last four years. She'd learned to be tough, to need no one.

And yet Khalil had been honest with her. He'd told her his story and she'd seen in his eyes that he'd wanted, even needed, her to believe him.

She took a deep breath. She thought of Andreas Markos and his determination to discredit her—her Council and country's desire for a king, or the closest thing to it. Her own foolish choices. 'It's complicated.'

'Most things are.'

He waited and Elena sifted through all the things she could say. 'My country, and my Council, would like a male ruler.'

'And you wanted that to be Aziz?'

She heard incredulity in his tone and bristled. 'Not like that. We had an agreement—he would attend state functions with me as Prince Consort, act as ruler in name only. It would satisfy the people and, I hoped, my Council. But he wouldn't actually have been involved in any decision making.'

'And you would have been satisfied with that?'

'It was what I wanted.'

'Why not find a man who could truly be your equal, your partner? Who could help you to rule, who could support you?'

Briefly, painfully, she thought of Paulo. 'You speak as though such a thing is simple. Easy.'

'No. Not that. But I wonder why you settle.'

She swallowed past the sudden tightness in her throat. 'What about you, Khalil? Do you want an equal, a partner in marriage as well as in ruling?'

Surprise flashed briefly in his eyes before his expression hardened. 'No.'

'Then why do you think I would want one? Simply because I am a woman?'

'No…' He gazed at her thoughtfully. 'I only asked, be-

cause if you needed to marry to please your country it seems
wise to pick a man who could be your friend and helpmate,
not a stranger.'

'Well, unfortunately for me, I don't have a friend and
helpmate waiting in the wings.' She'd meant to sound light
and wry but cringed at the self-pity she heard in her voice
instead. 'I've been alone for a long time,' she continued
when she trusted herself to sound more measured. 'I'm used
to it now, and it's more comfortable for me that way.' Even
if, since meeting Khalil, she'd started to realise all she'd
been missing out on. 'I imagine you might be the same.'

'Yes, I am.'

'Well, then.'

Khalil leaned back in his seat, his gaze sweeping over
her in thoughtful assessment. 'So you made this arrangement with Aziz to please your Council?'

'Appease them, more like.' Elena hesitated, not wanting
to admit more but knowing she needed to. 'The Head of
Council, Andreas Markos, has threatened to call a vote at
the next convening.' She took a breath, then forced herself
to finish. 'A vote to depose me and abolish the monarchy.'

Khalil was silent for a moment. 'And, let me guess, put
himself forward as head of state? Prime Minister, perhaps?'

Amazingly she found herself smiling wryly. 'Something like that.'

'And you think he won't if you are married?'

'I'm gambling that he won't,' Elena admitted. 'It's a
calculated risk.'

'I understand about those.'

'Yes, I suppose you do.' They smiled at each other, and
as the moment spun out Elena wondered at herself. How
could they be joking about her captivity? How could she
feel, in that moment, that they were co-conspirators, somehow complicit in all that had happened? Yet she did, and
more than that. So much more than that.

'The Thallian people like me, for the most part,' she

continued after a moment. 'And a royal marriage would be very popular. Markos would have a difficult time getting the Council to vote against me if the country approved.'

'I imagine,' Khalil said quietly, 'that your people like you very much indeed, Elena. I think you must be a good queen. You are clearly very loyal to your people.'

Pleasure rippled through her at the sincerity she heard in his voice. It meant so much, more than she'd ever even realised, to have someone believe in her.

'I'm trying to be a good queen,' she said in a low voice. 'I know I've made mistakes—' and she didn't want to talk about those '—but I love Thallia and its people. I want to celebrate its traditions, but also bring it into the twenty-first century.'

Khalil arched an eyebrow. 'And have you had much success so far?'

Elena ducked her head, suddenly shy. She wasn't used to talking about her accomplishments; so often they went unrecognised, by her Council, at any rate. 'A bit. I've introduced some new policies to protect women's rights. I've initiated a review of the national curriculum for primary schools. The education in Thallia has been one of its weaknesses.'

Khalil nodded, encouraging, and shyly Elena continued, 'I also helped to start an annual festival to celebrate the country's music and dance. It's a small thing, but important to our heritage. Thallia is named after the muse of poetry, you know.'

'I didn't know.' His eyes, Elena saw, crinkled when he smiled. She looked away.

'I know it doesn't sound like much.'

'Why belittle yourself or what you've done? There are enough people to do that for you. I've learned that much.'

'We've both persevered,' Elena said quietly. She met his gaze and held it, feeling an overwhelming solidarity with this man who had once been her enemy. They were so alike. He understood her, and she understood him, more than she'd ever expected.

'And this Markos,' Khalil said after a moment. 'He has that power—to call such a vote?'

'Unfortunately he does. Our Constitution states that the monarch cannot enact a law that isn't approved by the majority of the Council, and the Council can't pass one that isn't endorsed by the King or Queen.' Elena gave a rather bleak smile. 'But there's one important caveat: if the Council votes unanimously, the monarch is forced to acquiesce.'

'Even to your own demise?'

'That hasn't happened in a thousand years.' She looked away then, afraid he'd see the fear and shame on her face: the fear that she would be the one to end it. The shame that she wasn't strong enough to keep her crown or the promise she'd made to her father as he'd lain dying.

For Thallia, Elena. You must live for Thallia and the crown.

'You won't be the one to end it, Elena,' Khalil said quietly. The certainty in his voice made her glow inside. 'You're too strong for that.'

'Thank you,' she whispered.

'You have a lot of pressure put on you, for such a young woman,' Khalil continued. Elena just shrugged. 'You are an only child, I presume? The title has always fallen to you?'

'Yes, although for most of my childhood my parents hoped for more children.' Her mouth twisted downwards. 'For a boy.'

'And they were disappointed, I presume?'

'Yes. My mother had many miscarriages, but no more live children.'

'A tragedy.'

'Yes. I suppose it's why they felt a need to keep me so sheltered. Protected.'

'You were doted on?'

'Not exactly.' She thought of how little she'd actually

seen her parents. 'Kept apart, really. I didn't go to formal school until I was thirteen.' When she'd been gawky, overwhelmed and terribly shy. It hadn't been a great introduction to school life.

'And then you became Queen at a young age,' Khalil continued. He reached over to refill her glass with wine. Elena had already finished her first glass; Dutch courage, she supposed, for when she'd been telling him all that truth. She took another sip of wine now as she met his tawny gaze.

'Nineteen,' she said after she had swallowed, felt the liquid slip down her throat and steal seductively through her again.

'I know your parents died in a terrorist bombing,' Khalil said quietly. Elena nodded. She dreaded talking or even thinking about that awful day, hated the memories of the acrid smell of smoke, the stinging pain of broken glass on the palms of her hands, the ringing in her ears—all of it still causing her to wake up in an icy sweat far too many nights.

'I'm sorry,' Khalil continued. 'I know what it is to lose your parents when you are young.'

'Yes, I suppose you do.'

'You must miss them.'

'I do…'

Khalil cocked his head. 'You sound uncertain.'

'No, of course not.' Elena bit her lip. 'It's only that I didn't actually know them all that well. They were away so much… I miss the *idea* of them, if that makes sense. Of what—what I wish we could have been like as a family. That probably sounds strange.'

Khalil shook his head. 'Not strange at all,' he answered quietly, and Elena wondered if he missed the family he could have had too: loving parents, supporting him even now.

Khalil leaned forward, his fingers whispering against her cheek as he tucked a strand of hair behind her ear.

'You look so sad,' he said softly. 'I'm sorry to bring up bad memories.'

'It's okay,' she whispered. Khalil's fingers lingered on her cheek and she wished, suddenly and fiercely, that he wouldn't pull away.

That he would kiss her.

Her lips parted instinctively and her gaze rested on his mouth, making her realise yet again how sculpted and re-ally *perfect* his lips were. She wondered how they would feel. How they would taste. She'd never actually been kissed before, which suddenly seemed ridiculous at the age of twenty-three. But a convent-school education and becoming Queen at just nineteen had kept her from ever pursuing a romantic relationship. First there hadn't been any opportunity, and then she'd been so focused on protect-ing her crown and serving her country there hadn't been any time. Besides, suitable partners for a reigning queen were not exactly plentiful.

Elena knew she shouldn't be thinking of kissing Khalil now. With effort she dragged her gaze up towards his eyes, saw they were molten gold. His fingers tightened on her cheek, his thumb grazing her jawbone, drawing her inexo-rably forward. And Elena went, her heart starting to ham-mer as she braced herself for that wonderful onslaught.

Then Khalil released her, his hand falling away from her face as he sat back in his chair.

Her mind whirled with confusion and disappointment, and her body ached with unfulfilled desire. She scrambled for a way to cover her own obvious longing. 'This is very good,' she said stiltedly, gesturing to her half-eaten meal.

Khalil acknowledged her compliment with a nod. 'Thank you.'

'You have quite an elaborate set-up for a desert camp,' she continued, determined to keep the conversation off dangerous subjects—although every subject felt danger-ous now. Everything about Khalil felt dangerous.

Desirable.

'Comfort need not be sacrificed,' he remarked, taking a sip of wine.

'I suppose you feel very secure?' she asked. 'To have such a…permanent arrangement?'

'These are tents, Elena, as luxurious as they may be. My men and I could disassemble this camp in twenty minutes, if need be.'

'How do you know how to do all this if you grew up in America?'

'All this?' Khalil repeated, raising his eyebrows.

'Tents. Horses. Fighting. All this—this rebel stuff.' She realised she sounded rather ridiculous and she shrugged, half in apology, half in defiance. Heaven help her, she'd had two glasses of wine and she was nearly drunk.

'I served in the French Foreign Legion for seven years,' Khalil told her. 'I'm used to this kind of living.'

'You did?'

'It was good preparation.'

Everything in his life, Elena supposed, had been to prepare for being Sheikh, for taking the throne from the half-brother who didn't deserve it.

Aziz… Why could she barely remember his face now? She'd been going to marry him, yet she'd forgotten what he looked like, or how his voice sounded. And with that thought came another fast on its heels.

She wasn't going to marry him any more. Even if he rescued her, or Khalil released her, she wasn't going to marry Aziz.

It was both a revelation and completely unsurprising. Elena sat back, her mind spinning both from her thoughts and the wine she'd drunk. For the first time, she accepted her fate…even if she had no idea what it would actually mean for her title, her crown, her country.

'I'm not going to marry him,' she blurted. 'Aziz. Not even…not even if he found me in time.'

Something flashed in Khalil's eyes and he sat back. 'What made you change your mind?'

'You did,' she said simply, and she knew she meant it in more ways than one. Not just because he was the rightful Sheikh, but because he'd opened up feelings inside her she hadn't known she'd possessed. She couldn't marry Aziz now, couldn't settle for the kind of cold, mercenary arrangement she'd once wanted.

'I'm glad,' Khalil said quietly. They gazed at each other for a long moment, and everything in Elena tensed, yearned…

Then Khalil rose from the table. 'It is late. You should return to your tent.'

He reached for her hand, and Elena let him pull her up. She felt fluid, boneless; the wine must have really gone to her head.

He kept hold of her hand as they stepped outside the tent, the night dark and endless around them. The air was surprisingly cold and crisp, which had a sobering effect on Elena.

By the time they'd crossed the camp to her tent, Khalil's hand still loosely linked with hers, she wasn't feeling tipsy at all, just embarrassed. The evening's emotional intimacies and revelations were enough now to make her cringe.

'Goodnight, Elena.' Khalil stopped in front of her tent, sliding his hand from hers. He touched her chin with his fingers, tipped her head up so she was blinking at him, the night sky spangled with stars high above him.

For a moment as she looked up at him, just as when they'd been in his tent, she thought he might kiss her. Her lips parted and her head spun and her heart started thudding in a mix of alarm, anticipation and a suspended sense of wonder.

Khalil lowered his head, his mouth a whisper away from hers. 'Elena,' he murmured; it sounded like a question. Everything in Elena answered, *yes*.

She reached up to put her hands on his shoulders; her body pressed against his, the feel of his hard chest sending little shocks of sensation through her.

His hands slid up to frame her face, his fingers so gentle on her skin. She felt his desire as well as her own, felt his yearning and surprise, and thought, *We are alike in this too. We both want this, but we're also afraid to want it.*

Although perhaps Khalil didn't want it, after all, for he suddenly dropped his hands from her and stepped back. 'Goodnight,' he said again, and then he started walking back to his tent and was soon swallowed up by the darkness.

CHAPTER SIX

ELENA DIDN'T SEE Khalil at all the next day. She spent hours lying on her bed or sitting outside her tent, watching the men go about the camp and looking for Khalil.

She missed him. She told herself that was absurd, because she barely knew him. She'd only met him two days ago, and hardly in the best of circumstances.

Yet she still found herself reliving the times he'd touched her: the slide of his fingers on her jaw; the press of his chest against her cheek. She replayed their dinner conversation in her mind, thought about his lonely childhood, his determination to be Sheikh. And realised in just three days he would let her go and she would never see him again.

A thought that made a twist of bewildering longing spiral inside her.

Then the next morning Khalil came to her tent. He loomed large in the space and shamelessly she let her gaze rove over him, taking in his broad shoulders, his dark hair, his impossibly hard jaw.

'I need to go visit some of the desert tribes,' he told her without preamble. 'And I'd like you to go with me.'

Shock as well as a wary pleasure rippled through her in a double wave. 'You...would?'

He arched an eyebrow and gave her a small smile. 'Wouldn't you like to see something other than the inside of this tent?'

'Yes, but...why do you want me to go?' A terrible suspicion took hold of her. 'You aren't…you aren't going to show me off as some trophy of war, are you? Show your people how you captured Aziz's bride?' Just the idea made her stomach churn. Why *shouldn't* he do such a thing? He'd captured her, after all. She was his possession, his prize.

Khalil's face darkened, his eyebrows drawing together in a fierce frown. 'No, of course not. In any case, the people I'm visiting wouldn't be impressed by such antics.'

'Wouldn't they?'

'They are loyal to me. And I would never act in such a barbaric fashion.'

'Then why are you taking me?'

Khalil stared at Elena, the question reverberating through him. *Then why are you taking me?*

The simple answer was because he wanted to. Because he'd been thinking about her since they'd had dinner together, since she'd shown how she believed him. Believed *in* him. And having someone's trust, even if it was just a little of it, was as heady and addictive as a drug. He wanted more. He wanted more of Elena and he wanted more of the person he felt he was in her eyes. The man he wanted to be.

The realisation had kept him from her for an entire day, fighting it, fighting the need and the desire, the danger and the weakness of wanting another person. Of opening himself to pain, loss and grief.

By last night he'd convinced himself that taking her to see the desert tribes who supported him was a political move; it would strengthen his position to have Aziz's former bride on his side.

Gazing at her now, her hair tumbled over her shoulders, her heavy-lidded eyes with their perceptive grey-gold gaze trained on him, he knew he'd been fooling himself.

This wasn't some political manoeuvre. This was simply him wanting to be with Elena.

'I'm taking you,' he said, choosing his words slowly,

carefully, 'because I want you to meet the people who support me.'

Her eyes widened. Her lips parted and then curved in a tremulous smile. 'You do?'

Khalil's hands curled into fists. Everything in him resisted this admission, this appalling weakness. Where was his ruthless determination now? All he wanted in this moment was to see Elena's smile deepen. 'I do.'

'All right,' she said, and Khalil felt relief and even joy pour through him. He smiled, a wider smile than he'd ever felt on his face before, and she grinned back.

Something had changed. Something was changing right here between them and, God help him, but he couldn't stop it. He didn't even want to.

'We should leave within the hour. Can you ride?'

'Yes.'

'Then dress for riding. Leila will find you the appropriate clothes.' With a nod, he started to leave, then turned back to face her. 'Thank you, Elena,' he said quietly, meaning it utterly, and the smile she offered him felt like a precious gift.

An hour later Elena met him on the edge of the camp, where he was saddling the horses they would take. Khalil nodded his approval of her sensible clothing, headscarf and boots, a familiar tightness in his chest easing just at the sight of her.

'We should waste no time in departing. It is half a day's ride and I intend for us to arrive before nightfall.'

She glanced, clearly surprised, at the two horses. 'We're going alone?'

'Three men will accompany us, but they will ride separately. We will meet up with the guards before we enter the camp, so all will be appropriate.'

'Appropriate?'

'In the desert, a man and woman generally do not ride alone.'

She nodded slowly, accepting, her gaze darting between the horses and him.

Khalil acknowledged he was breaching protocol in so many ways. 'You'll be safe with me, Elena,' he said and she looked back at him.

'I know that.'

'Do you?' He felt a smile spread across his face. 'Good.'

'I trust you,' she said simply, and for a moment he couldn't speak. He'd kidnapped her, after all. He didn't deserve her trust, yet she gave it. Freely. Wholly.

'Thank you,' he finally said.

She stepped closer to him, so he caught the scent of roses. 'Are we travelling alone because it's safer? I mean, so Aziz won't find us?'

She spoke without any rancour, yet Khalil felt that churning guilt once more, and more acutely this time, because for the first time something felt stronger than his burning need to be Sheikh.

He refused to name just what it was.

'Yes,' he answered. 'Does that…distress you?'

Her clear gaze searched his and she smiled wryly. 'Not as much as it should.'

He acknowledged her point with a small nod. 'Things are changing.'

'They've already changed,' she said quietly, and something in him both swelled and ached.

He shouldn't want things to change. Change meant losing his focus, losing his whole sense of self. What was he, if not the future Sheikh of Kadar? Everything in his life had been for that purpose. He'd had no room for other ideas or ambitions, and certainly none for relationships.

Yet he knew Elena was right. Things had already changed…whether he'd wanted them to or not.

'Let's go,' he said, a bit more gruffly than he intended, and he laced his fingers together to offer Elena a foothold.

She rode just like she walked or stood, with inherent

elegance and pride. Her back was ramrod straight as she controlled the excited prancing of her horse.

'How well can you ride?' he asked and her eyes sparkled at him.

'Well.'

Khalil's mouth curved. 'Let's see about that,' he said, and with a shout he took off at a gallop. He heard Elena's surprised laughter echo behind him as she gave chase.

Elena felt the kind of thrill of exhilaration she hadn't experienced since she'd been a child riding in Thallia as she followed Khalil. It felt wonderful to be on a horse again, the desert flashing by in a blur of rocks and sand. She had had no time for such pursuits since she'd been queen. She hadn't ridden like this in years.

The only sound was her horse's hooves galloping across the sand. She spurred the beast on, eager to catch up with Khalil—or even pass him. Although he hadn't said, she knew it had become a race.

Glancing behind him, Khalil pointed to a towering, needle-like boulder in the distance that Elena knew must be the finish line. She nodded back and crouched low over the horse as the wind whistled past. She was only a length behind him, and in the last dash to the finish line she made up half a length, but Khalil's horse still crossed a beat before hers.

Laughing, she reined the animal in and patted his sweat-soaked neck. 'That was close.'

'Very close,' Khalil agreed. His teeth gleamed white in his bronzed face. He wore a turban to keep out the sun and sand, and somehow it made him look more masculine. More desirable. 'Foolish, perhaps, to race,' he continued. 'There is a small oasis here. We'll let the horses drink before we continue.'

'A small oasis? I'd thought the next one was a day's ride by camel.'

Khalil just shrugged and Elena let out a huff of indignation. 'So you lied to me?'

'I wanted to discourage you from doing something foolish, something that most certainly wouldn't end well.'

'I could have escaped now,' Elena pointed out. 'I was on a horse, with water and food in my saddlebags.'

Khalil gazed at her evenly. 'I know. But you didn't.'

'No.' She hadn't even thought of it, hadn't been remotely tempted. The knowledge should have shamed her, but instead she felt almost ebullient.

They led the horses to the oasis, and as the animals drank Khalil gazed at the horizon with a frown.

'What's wrong?' Elena asked.

'It looks like a storm might rise.'

'A storm?' She gazed up at the endless blue sky, hard and bright, in incredulity. 'How on earth can you tell?'

'Look there.' Khalil pointed to the horizon and Elena squinted. She could see a faint grey smudge, but that was all. If Khalil hadn't pointed it out, she wouldn't have noticed it.

'Surely that's far away.'

'It is now. Storms in the desert can travel all too quickly. We should ride. I want to get to the camp before the storm gets to us. We'll need to meet up with the guards as well.'

They saddled up once more and headed off at a brisk canter. The sun was hot above, the sand shimmering in the midday heat. Elena kept her gaze on the horizon, noticing with each passing hour that the faint smudge was becoming darker and wider. The stiff breeze she'd felt at camp had turned into a relentless wind.

After several hours of tense riding, Khalil guided them to a grouping of boulders. 'We will not be able to outride the storm,' he said. 'We'll have to shelter here for the night and try to meet up with my men in the morning.'

Elena slid off her horse, glancing at the forbidding-looking rocks with some apprehension. 'Where are we, exactly?'

Khalil gave her the glimmer of a smile. 'In the middle of the desert.'

'Yes…' Standing there next to her horse, the desert endless around her, the sky darkening rapidly and the wind kicking up sand, she suddenly felt acutely how strange this all was. How little she knew Khalil, even if her heart protested otherwise.

'Elena.' Khalil stood in front of her and she blinked up at him, nearly swaying on her feet. 'I will keep you safe.'

She believed him, Elena knew. She trusted him, even if it was foolish. When had any other person been concerned for her safety? Paulo had said he had, but he'd been lying. Her father had, but only for the sake of his country, and he'd paid with his life.

Looking up at Khalil, Elena was struck as forcefully as a fist with the knowledge that he would keep her safe because he cared for her as a person, not as a pawn, or even as a queen. Simply because of who she was—and who he was. The knowledge nearly brought tears to her eyes.

'You look as if you are going to collapse,' he said gently. 'Come. I have food and drink.' He took her by the hand, his warm, callused palm comforting as it closed around her own far smaller one, and led her towards the group of immense black boulders.

He was clearly familiar with the territory, for he led her with confidence through the maze of rocks, coming to a stop in front of a large, flat rock sheltered by a huge boulder above it.

He drew her underneath it and she sat down with her back against the boulder, the overhanging rock providing shelter from the rising wind and swirling sand. He removed his turban so she pulled off her headscarf and ran a hand over her dishevelled hair.

'Drink,' he said and handed her a canteen of water.

She unscrewed the top of the canteen and took a much-needed and grateful sip of water.

'And there's food,' Khalil said, handing her a piece of flat bread and some dried meat. She ate both, as did he, both of them silently chewing as the wind picked up and howled around them.

After she'd finished eating Elena drew her knees up to her chest and watched Khalil put the remnants of their meal back in the saddlebags.

He was a beautiful man, she thought, not for the first time; his sculpted mouth and long lashes softened a face of utterly unyielding hardness. As he tidied up she saw several whitened scars on the inside of his wrist and she leaned forward.

'How did you get those?'

Khalil tensed, his mouth thinning. 'Rope burns,' he said shortly, and Elena stared at him in confusion.

'Rope?'

'It was a long time ago.' He turned away, clearly not wanting to say anything further, although Elena wanted to ask. She wanted to know. Rope burns on his wrists… Had he been *tied up*?

She sat back against the rock and watched as he settled himself opposite her. 'Now what?' she asked.

His smile gleamed in the oncoming darkness. 'Well, I'm afraid I didn't bring a chessboard.'

She gave a little laugh. 'Pity. I'm actually quite good at chess.'

'So am I.'

'Is that a challenge?'

His gaze flicked over her. 'Maybe.'

Excitement fizzed through her. Were they actually flirting? About *chess*? 'Perhaps we'll have a match some time,' she said, and realised belatedly how that made it sound— as if they would have some kind of future beyond her time here. Even though she'd accepted she wouldn't marry Aziz, it didn't mean she had any kind of future with Khalil. She'd be deluding herself to think otherwise.

In two days he was going to let her go.

Why did that make her feel so…*bereft*?

'What are you thinking about?' Khalil asked quietly and she turned back to him, wondering if she dared to admit the truth.

'That in two days I might never see you again.' She took a breath, held it, and forced herself to continue. 'I don't like that thought, Khalil.'

She couldn't make out his expression in the darkness. 'Elena,' he said, and it sounded like a warning.

'I know this is going to sound ridiculous,' she continued, *needing* to be honest now, 'but you're the first real friend I've ever had.'

She tensed, waiting for incredulity, perhaps his discomfort or even derision. Instead he looked away and said quietly, 'That's not ridiculous. In many ways, you're the first friend I've had too.'

Her breath caught in her chest. 'Really?'

He turned back to her, the glimmer of a smile just visible in the moonlight. 'Really.'

'Not even at school? In America?'

She felt him tense but then he shook his head. 'Not even then. What about you? No school friends?'

'Not really.' She hugged her knees to her chest, remembering those lonely years in convent school. 'I was terribly shy in school, coming to it so late. And, looking back, I think the fact that I was a princess intimidated the other girls, although at the time I was the one who was intimidated. Everyone else made it look so easy. Having friends, having a laugh. I envied them all. I wanted to be like they were, but I didn't know how. And then later, after school…' She thought for one blinding moment of Paulo and her throat tightened. 'Sometimes it just doesn't seem worth the risk.'

'The risk?'

She swallowed and met his gaze unflinchingly. It was amazing how easy, how *necessary,* honesty felt sometimes. 'Of getting hurt.'

Khalil didn't speak for a long moment. Okay, so honesty wasn't so easy, Elena thought as she shifted where she sat. She had no idea what he felt about what she'd said.

'Have you been hurt, Elena?' he finally asked, and in the darkness his voice seemed like a separate entity, as soft as velvet, caressing the syllables of her name.

'Hasn't everyone, at one time or another?'

'That's not really an answer.'

'Have *you* been hurt, Khalil?'

'That's not an answer either, but yes, I have.' He spoke evenly, but she still felt the ocean of pain underneath. 'My father hurt me when he chose to disown and banish me.'

'Oh, Khalil.' She bit her lip, remorse rushing through her. 'I'm sorry. That was a thoughtless question for me to ask.'

'Not at all. But I want you to answer my question. What were you talking about when you said friendship wasn't worth the risk?'

'I had a friend once,' Elena said slowly. 'And he let me down rather badly. He—betrayed me.' She shook her head. 'That sounds melodramatic, but that's what happened.'

'He,' Khalil said neutrally, and with a dart of surprise she wondered if he was actually jealous.

'Yes, he. But it wasn't romantic, not remotely.' She sighed. 'It was stupid, really. I was stupid to trust him.'

'So this man is why you don't trust people?'

'I've learned my lesson. But I trust you, Khalil.'

She heard his breath come out in a rush. 'Maybe you shouldn't.'

'Why do you say that?'

'Do I need to remind you why you're here in the first place, Elena? I *kidnapped* you.'

She heard genuine remorse in his voice and she reached out and touched his hand, her fingers skimming across his skin. 'I know you did, Khalil, but I also understand why you did it.'

'You're justifying my actions to me?' he asked with a wry laugh, and Elena managed a laugh back.

'I don't know what I'm doing,' she answered honestly. 'And I don't know what I'd do if you let me go right now. I don't know how I'd feel.'

She held her breath, waiting for his reply, needing him to say something—but what?

'I don't know how I'd feel either,' Khalil answered in a low voice, and that was enough. That was more than enough.

Whatever was happening between them, Khalil recognised it as well. Just as he'd said before, *things were changing.*

Things had changed.

'The temperature is dropping,' Khalil said after a moment. 'Here.' He handed her a blanket and Elena wrapped it around herself. The wind howled; the night air was cold and crisp as she huddled against the rock, trying to make herself comfortable.

After a moment she heard Khalil sigh. 'Elena. Come here.'

'Come—where?'

'Here.' He patted his lap. 'You're obviously cold and I know of only one way to warm you right now.'

Her cheeks heated as she thought of other ways he could warm her. Ways she'd never even experienced before. 'But...'

'You've been on my lap before,' he reminded her.

Yes, and she'd enjoyed it far too much. Elena hesitated, torn between the fierce desire to be close to Khalil again and the ever-present need to keep herself safe. What could happen between them, after all? In two days she would return to Thallia, and without a husband. If she had any sense, she'd keep her distance from Khalil.

It seemed she didn't have any sense. She scooted across the rock, hesitating in front of him, not quite sure actually how to get on his lap.

Khalil had no such hesitation. Without ceremony or any awkwardness at all he slid his arms around her waist and hauled her onto him. Once there, she found it amazingly easy to curl into him just as she'd done before, her legs lying across his, her cheek pressed against his chest.

'Now that's better,' Khalil said, and his voice was a comforting rumble she could feel reverberate right through her. He stroked her hair, his fingers smoothing over the dark strands.

'Sleep,' he said, his voice a caress, and obediently she closed her eyes even though she knew she would be less likely to sleep warm and safe on Khalil's lap than when she'd been huddling by herself in the cold.

She was too aware of everything: the solid strength of his chest, the steady rise and fall of his breathing. The warmth of him, his arms snuggled safely around her, and even the scent of him, a woodsy aftershave mingled with the smell of horse and leather.

He continued to stroke her hair, pulling her gently into his chest so she snuggled in even more deeply, her lips barely brushing the warm, bare skin of his throat. Never had anything felt so familiar. So right.

She slept.

And woke in the clutches of a nightmare.

She hadn't had one of her old nightmares in a long time, mainly because she never slept deeply enough to have any dreams at all. Now lulled to sleep in the warmth and safety of Khalil's arms, it came for her.

Smoke. Screams. Blood. Bombs. In her dreams it was always the same: a chaos of terror, bodies strewn over the floor, shattered glass cutting into her palms. And the worst part of all: the heavy weight of her father on her back, his body shielding hers from the explosion, the last words he ever spoke whispered into her ear along with his last breath.

'For Thallia.'

'Elena. *Elena.*'

She came to consciousness with Khalil's hands on her shoulders, shaking her gently, and tears on her face. She drew a shuddering breath and felt panic clutch at her even though she was awake, for the darkness and the howling wind reminded her of that terrible night.

'It was just a dream, Elena.' She felt Khalil's hands slide up to cup her face, his forehead pressing into hers as if he could imbue her with his warmth, his certainty. 'Whatever it was, it was just a dream.'

She closed her eyes, willing her heart rate to slow, the terrible images that flashed through her mind in brutal replay to fade. 'I know,' she whispered after a long moment. 'I know.'

The touch of his palm cradling her cheek felt achingly, painfully sweet. 'What do you dream of, Elena?' he whispered and her throat went tight, too tight to speak. He ran his thumb lightly over her lips. 'What haunts you so?'

'Memories,' she managed, her voice choked, suffocated. She reached up to wipe the remnants of tears from her face. 'Memories of when my parents died.'

Khalil's hands stilled on her face. 'You were there?'

'Yes.'

'Why didn't I know that?'

'It was kept out of the press, out of respect for my family. That's what I wanted. It was hard enough, dealing with what had happened, without everyone gawking at me.'

'Yes.' Khalil slid his arms around her and pulled her closer to him. 'I can imagine it was. Do you want to talk about it?'

Amazingly, she did. Normally she never talked about her parents' deaths to anyone. She didn't even like remembering it. But, safe in Khalil's arms, she felt the need to tell him her story. Share her pain.

'You know they died in the bombing,' Elena began slowly. 'And as far as I know, my mother died instantly. But my father—my father and I were alive after the bomb went off.'

Khalil didn't say anything, just held her close. After a moment Elena continued. 'I can't remember much after the first bomb went off. I was thrown across the room and I landed on my back. I must have been unconscious for a little while, because I remember waking up, feeling completely disorientated. And everything...' She drew a shuddering breath. 'Everything was madness. People screaming and crying. So much blood...' She shook her head, closing her eyes as she pressed her face into the solid warmth of Khalil's chest.

'I crawled across the floor, looking for my parents. There was broken glass everywhere but I didn't even feel it, although later I saw my hands were covered in blood. It was so strange, so surreal... I felt numb and yet utterly terrified. And then I found my mother...' She stopped then, because she never let herself think about that moment even though sometimes she felt as if it never left her thoughts: her mother's lifeless face, her mouth opened in a soundless scream, her staring eyes.

She'd turned from her mother's body and had seen her father stumbling towards her, terror etched on every feature.

'There was a second bomb,' she told Khalil, her voice muffled against his chest. 'My father knew somehow. Maybe he guessed, or saw something. But he ran towards me and threw his body over me as it went off. The last thing he said...' Another deep, shuddering breath. '"For Thallia",' she quoted softly. 'He said "For Thallia" because he was saving my life for our country, so I could be queen.'

Khalil was silent for a long moment, his arms snugged

around her. 'And you think that was the only reason he was saving your life,' he surmised quietly. 'For the monarchy, not for you. Not because you were his daughter. Because he loved you.'

His words, so softly and surely spoken, cut her to the heart, because she knew they were true and she was amazed that Khalil had been able to see that. Understand it.

'I never knew what they felt,' she whispered. 'I hardly ever saw them, all through my childhood. They were devoted to Thallia, but they never spent time with me.' She let out a shuddering breath. 'And then they were gone in a single moment, and I didn't know if I missed them because they were dead or because I never actually knew them in the first place.' She closed her eyes. 'Is that awful?'

'No, it's understandable.'

'But it seems so ungrateful. My father gave his life for me.'

'You've a right to your feelings, Elena. They loved you, but how were you to know it if they didn't show it until they'd died?'

She pressed her face even harder against his chest, willing the tears that threatened to recede. She wasn't even sure what she was crying for. Her parents' deaths? The lack of relationship she'd had while they'd been alive? Or simply the swamping sense of loss she felt, as if she'd experienced it for ever?

Until Khalil.

She twisted to look up at him. 'I've never told anyone all that.'

'I'm glad you told me.'

'I'm glad I did too.' She hesitated, because she felt a need to reassure him and, perhaps herself, that she knew this wasn't real—that whatever intimacy had sprung between them was separate from what was going on in their lives. It didn't really count.

Yet she said nothing, because it *felt* like it counted. It

felt like the only thing that counted. Khalil had given her something, or maybe he'd just showed her she already had it: a capacity to share, to trust. To love.

She looked up at him, searching his face, wanting to know what he was feeling, if he felt the same pull of attraction and empathy that she did. But then she met his gaze and saw the fire burning there and her breath caught in her chest as desire, raw, fierce and overwhelming, crashed over her.

His face was so close to hers she could feel his breath fanning against her cheek, see the dark glint of stubble on his chin. His lips were no more than a whisper away from hers and, as she stared up at him and heard his breath hitch, she knew without a doubt she wanted to close that small distance between their mouths.

She wanted him to kiss her.

His head dipped and her heart seemed to stop and then soar. His lips were so close now that if she moved at all they would be touching his. They would be kissing.

Yet she didn't move, transfixed as she was by both wonder and fear, and Khalil didn't move either.

The moment stretched between them, suspended, endless.

His breath came out in a shudder and his hands tightened around her face. She tried to say something but words eluded her; all she could do was feel. Want.

Then with another shuddering breath he closed that small space between their mouths and his lips touched hers in her first and most wonderful kiss.

She let out a tiny sigh both of satisfaction and surrender, her hands coming up to tangle in the surprising softness of his hair. Her lips parted and Khalil deepened the kiss, pulling her closer as his tongue delved into her mouth, and everything in Elena throbbed powerfully to life.

She'd never known you could feel like this, want like this. It was so intense and sweet it almost felt painful. She pressed against him, acting on an instinct she hadn't re-alised she possessed. Khalil slid his hand from her face to cup her breast, and a shocked gasp escaped her mouth as exquisite sensation darted through her.

Khalil withdrew, dropping his hand and easing back from her so she felt a rush of loss. He reached up to cover her hands with his own and draw them down to her own lap.

'I shouldn't have...' he began then shook his head. Even in the moonlit darkness she could see the regret and re-morse etched on his harsh features.

'I wanted you to,' she blurted and he just shook his head again.

'You should sleep again, if you can,' he said quietly and Elena bit her lip, blinking hard. She wondered, with a rush of humiliation, if she'd actually been the one to kiss him. In that moment it had been hard to tell, and she'd wanted it so much...

Had she actually thrown herself at him?

'Sleep, Elena,' he said softly, and he repositioned her on his lap so her head was once again pillowed by his chest. He stroked her hair just as he had before and Elena closed her eyes, even though sleep seemed farther away than ever.

What had just happened? And how could she feel so unbearably, overwhelmingly disappointed?

CHAPTER SEVEN

DAWN BROKE OVER the dunes, turning the sand pink with pale sunlight. The storm had died down and the desert had reshaped itself into a new landscape of drifts and dunes. Leaving Elena sleeping in their rocky shelter, Khalil went to check on the horses and get his bearings.

And also to figure out just what he was going to say to her when she awoke.

That kiss had been completely unplanned. Incredibly sweet. And it had left Khalil in an extremely uncomfortable state of arousal for the rest of the night.

He hadn't been able to sleep with Elena on his lap, her hair brushing his cheek, her soft body relaxed and pliant against his. His whole body, his whole *self*, had been in a state of unbearable awareness, exquisite agony.

Sleep had been the farthest thing from his mind.

But now, in the cold light of day, reality returned with an almighty thud. He could not act on his attraction to Elena. He could not nurture any softer feelings for her. He had a goal, a plan, and neither included the Queen of Thallia beyond keeping her captive and then letting her go.

Except, somehow he had forgotten that when he'd held her in his lap. When he'd shared dinner with her in his tent, and invited her to accompany him to visit the desert tribes. When he'd encouraged her to share about her life, and had told her a little bit about his. When he'd let her into his mind and even his heart. *When he'd kissed her.*

He'd told her things had changed, and he felt the change in himself. He was losing sight of his priorities and chasing rainbows instead. How could he be such a fool? How could he let his focus slip, even for a second?

It was time to get back on track, Khalil knew. To forget the fanciful feelings he'd been harbouring for Elena. What an idiot he was, to feel something soft even for a moment! To trust her. Care for her. It would only end badly… in so many ways. He knew that from hard experience. He wasn't about to repeat the mistake of trusting someone, loving someone.

Not that he loved her, Khalil told himself quickly. He barely knew her. Things had become intense between them because they were in an intense situation, that was all.

He let out a long, low breath and headed for the horses. The animals had weathered last night's storm well enough and were happy for Khalil to feed and water them. He'd just finished and was turning back to check on Elena when he saw her standing between the towering black rocks, looking tired and pale, yet also tall and straight…and so very beautiful.

His gut tightened. His groin ached. And as he stood and stared at her he was reminded of her nightmare, of the vulnerability she'd shown and the secrets she'd shared. He thought of her witnessing the death of her parents, the utter horror of the terrorist attack, and a howl of need to protect her rose up inside him. In that moment last night he'd almost told her his own terrible memories. Laid bare his own secrets.

Almost.

Now he pushed the memories away and gave her a measured smile. 'Good morning. Are you rested?'

'A bit.' She took a step closer to him and he saw uncertainty in her eyes. Questions loomed there that he didn't want her to ask. Had no intention of answering, not even in the seething silence of his own mind.

'We can eat and then we should ride. The settlement we've been aiming for is only another hour or so from here, and I hope my men will be waiting for us there. We can explain to the tribe how we became separated in the storm.'

She nodded slowly, her gaze sweeping over him like a sorrowful searchlight. Khalil tried not to flinch under it; that guilt was coming back, along with a powerful desire to pull her into his arms and bury his face in her hair, to comfort her—and himself.

What a joke. He was the last person qualified to give or receive comfort. The last person to think of caring or being cared for. He half-regretted taking her on this god-forsaken trip; he wished he'd left her to stew in her tent. But only half, because even now, when he knew better and had told himself so, he was still glad to see her. Was glad she was here with him.

'Come,' he said, and beckoned her back towards their rocky shelter. They ate the remaining flat bread and dried meat in silence, and then Khalil saddled the horses while Elena watched.

A moment later they were riding across the desert, the sky hard and blue above them, the air dry, and becoming hotter by the minute.

He watched her out of the corner of his eye, admired her long, straight back, the proud tilt of her head. She would never be bowed, he thought with a surge of almost possessive admiration. She would never allow herself the possibility of defeat. Looking at her now reminded him of how it had felt to hold her: the soft press of her breasts against his chest; the way her hair had brushed his cheek; the smell of her, like rosewater and sunshine.

His horse veered suddenly to avoid a rock, startling Khalil, and he swore under his breath. Already he was losing his concentration again, forgetting his focus. All because of Elena.

Not that he could blame her for his own lack of control. No, he blamed himself, and this sudden need that opened up inside him like a great, yawning chasm of emptiness longing to be filled. He wasn't used to feeling such a thing; for thirty years he'd basically been on his own. The only person he'd let close in all that time was Dimah, and that relationship had had its own problems and pitfalls.

No, he wasn't used to this at all. And he didn't like it. At all.

Liar.

Two hours after starting off, they finally rode into a small Bedouin settlement on the edge of an oasis. There had been no sight of his men, and uneasily Khalil wondered how it would look to the Sheikh for him to ride in alone with Elena. He pushed the thought from his mind. There was nothing he could do about it now.

He'd been here once before on one of his tours of duty through the desert, getting to know the people he was meant to rule, rallying support. Much to his amazement, they had welcomed him.

Such a response still surprised him after all these years: that anyone could accept him. Want him.

Yet he still didn't trust it, because he knew all too well how the people you loved, the people you thought loved you back, could turn on you. Utterly.

Several men came up as he swung off the horse, offering their greetings and taking the horses away before leading Khalil to the Sheikh's tent. He glanced back at Elena who was looking pale but composed as several women hustled her off to another tent.

Deciding she could handle herself for the moment, Khalil went to greet the tribe's Sheikh and explain why he was here. It would be better, he knew, to leave Elena alone for a while.

For ever.

* * *

Several clucking women surrounded Elena and she was carried along with them to a tent, bemused by their interest, and more than a little hurt by the stony look she'd seen on Khalil's face as he'd turned away.

So he regretted their kiss last night. Clearly. And she should regret it too; of course she should. Kissing Khalil was a very bad idea. Caring about him was even worse.

The trouble was, she couldn't regret it. She ached with longing for another kiss—and more. For *him*.

She'd come to this desert tribe because she'd wanted to, because she wanted to see the people who cared about Khalil.

As she cared about him.

More, it seemed, than he wanted her to.

Once in the tent, the women fluttered around her like colourful, chattering birds, touching her hair, her cheek, the clothes she wore that were now grimed with dust and dirt. Elena didn't understand anything they said, and it appeared none of them spoke either English or Greek, the two languages in which she was fluent. They all seemed wonderfully friendly, though, and she let herself be carried along by the wave of their enthusiasm as they fetched her fresh clothing and led her down to the oasis where the women of the village bathed.

After a moment's hesitation at the water's edge, she took off her clothes as the other women were doing and immersed herself in the warm, silky water. After a night in the desert and hours of hard riding it felt wonderful to wash the dirt from her body, scrub the sand from her scalp. She enjoyed the camaraderie of the women too, watching as they chattered, laughed and splashed, utterly at ease with one another. She was gratified by their willingness to include her even though she was a stranger who didn't even speak their language.

After she had bathed she slipped on the unfamiliar garments the women gave her: a cotton chemise and then a loose, woven dress with wide sleeves embroidered with red and yellow. She left her hair down to dry in the sun and accompanied the women back up to the camp where a meal had been laid out.

She looked for Khalil, and tried to ignore the flicker of disappointment she felt when she could not find him.

In the camp the women ushered her into their circle and plied her with a delicious stew of lentils, flat bread and cardamom-flavoured coffee similar to what she had drunk with Khalil. As they ate and chatted, they mimed questions which Elena did her best to answer in a similar fashion.

Within an hour or two she felt herself start to fade, the exhaustion from the night spent outside and the endless hours on horseback making her eyelids begin to droop. The women noticed and, laughing, brought her to a make-shift bed piled high with woven blankets. Grateful for their concern, Elena lay down in it, and her last thought before sleep claimed her was of Khalil.

She woke the next morning to bright sunlight filtering through the flaps of the tent that was now empty save for herself. Today, she acknowledged with a heaviness she knew she shouldn't feel, was the last day of her imprisonment. Aziz's six weeks were up. He would have married someone else or forfeited his title. Either way, she wasn't needed, and Khalil could let her go.

A thought that mere days ago would have brought relief and even joy, not this sick plunging in her stomach. She didn't want to leave Khalil, and she didn't want to face her country and Council alone. How would she explain what had happened? She supposed she'd go with what Khalil had originally suggested: 'a necessary detainment'. Perhaps she would tell the Council she'd changed her mind about the marriage when she realised Aziz's claim to the throne wasn't legitimate.

She spared a second's thought then for the man she'd

intended to marry, a moment's regret. He'd been kind to her. Looking back, she saw how his easy charm had hidden a deeper part of himself, something dark, perhaps painful. What had his experience of Khalil's banishment, his sudden arrival at the palace, felt like? How had it affected him? She supposed she would never know.

Just as she would never truly know Khalil. She'd had glimpses of a man who was both tender and strong, who had the ruthless determination to kidnap a monarch but the gentleness to cradle her and wipe away her tears. A man she knew she now cared about, whom she might never see again after today.

Sighing, Elena swung her legs onto the floor and combed her hands through her tangled hair, wondering where everyone was and just what this day would bring.

When she was as presentable as she could make herself, she stepped outside the tent, blinking in the bright sunlight. People bustled around the camp, busy with various tasks and chores; she could not see Khalil.

A woman from the night before approached her with a smile and gestured for her to come forward. Elena followed her, stopping suddenly as she caught sight of Khalil talking with a group of men. The woman followed Elena's transfixed gaze and giggled, saying something Elena didn't understand, but she had an uncomfortable feeling she'd got the gist of.

This was confirmed a few moments later when Khalil broke apart from the men to join her by a fire where she'd been eating some bread and tahini for breakfast.

'Good morning.'

She nodded back her own greeting, her mouth full of bread and her cheeks starting to heat. It was ridiculous, to have this kind of reaction to him, but it was also undeniable. All she could picture was the look of both tenderness and hunger on his face right before he'd kissed her. All she could remember was how wonderful it had felt—and how much more she had wanted.

Still did.

'You slept well?'

She swallowed her mouthful of bread and nodded once more. 'Yes, I was exhausted.'

'Understandable.'

His expression was unreadable, his tawny eyes veiled, and Elena had a terrible feeling he was going to leave it at that. Something that had become almost easy between them now felt stilted and awkward. Which was, she acknowledged, perhaps as it should be, and yet...

She felt the loss.

'What happens now?' she asked, more just to keep the conversation going than any real desire to know, although she should *want* to know, considering this was her future. Her life. She forced herself to say the words that had been throbbing through her since she'd woken that morning. 'The six weeks are up.'

'I know.'

She gazed up at him, tried to read his expression, but he looked utterly impassive. 'Are you going to let me go?'

'I promised I would.'

She nodded jerkily, feeling bereft and unable to keep herself from it.

'We should stay here for another night, if you are amenable. There is a wedding in the tribe and a big celebration is planned this evening.' He hesitated, and it almost looked as if he were blushing. 'We are the guests of honour.'

'We are? I could understand why you might be, but—'

'The members of the tribe are under the impression that we are newly married,' he interjected in a low voice. 'I have not corrected it.'

'What?' Elena bolted upright, gaping at him before she could think to close her mouth. So that was why the woman had looked at Khalil and giggled. 'But why are they under that impression?' she asked, her voice coming out in something close to a squeak. 'And why haven't you corrected it?'

'They are under it because it is the only reason they know of why a man and woman would be travelling alone together. If the storm hadn't arisen, we would have entered the camp with my men—'

'But couldn't you have explained about the storm?'

'That would not have been a good enough reason. The desert tribes are traditional. I didn't explain because to do so would have brought disapproval and shame upon both of us.' His mouth and eyes both hardened. 'Something I should have considered more carefully. I acted foolishly in asking you to accompany me.'

Elena blinked, trying to hide the hurt his recrimination made her feel. He regretted her company, along with that kiss. She drew a breath, forced herself to think about the practicalities. 'And what happens when they discover we're not married?'

'Ideally, they won't. At least, not while we're here.'

'Eventually, though…'

'Eventually, yes. But by that time I will be installed as Sheikh and I will be able to make any apologies or explanations that are necessary. To do so right now would invite even more instability.' He sighed, shifting his weight restlessly. 'I admit, I don't like lying, not even by silence—but this is a critical time, not just for myself, but for Kadar. The less unrest there is, the better.'

'So I am meant to pretend to be your wife?' Elena asked, her voice a hushed and disbelieving whisper.

Khalil's gaze seemed to burn into hers. 'Only for one day and night. Will that be so hard, Elena?'

She felt her body flood with warmth, her face flush. No, it wouldn't be hard at all—that was the problem. She looked away, willing her blush to recede. 'I don't like lying,' she muttered.

'Nor do I. But there is no choice. Although I would have

hoped that such a pretence would not be quite so abhorrent to you.' His eyes glowed with both knowledge and memory, reminding her of their kiss. It felt as if he were taunting her that he knew she wanted him, that such a fantasy would not be unpleasant at all but far, far too desirable.

Elena broke their locked gaze first, looking away from all the knowledge in Khalil's eyes. 'And after tonight?' she asked when she trusted her voice to sound as level as his had been. 'Then you'll let me go?'

'Yes. I'll take you to Siyad myself. Now that Aziz will be forced to call a referendum, there is no need for me to remain in the desert.'

She swallowed, her mind spinning with all this new information. 'What will happen to Aziz?'

Khalil shrugged. 'He will return to Europe, I imagine. He has a house in Paris. He can live the playboy life he so enjoys.'

'That's not fair,' Elena protested. 'He might be a playboy, but he has his own business, and he's done a lot of good—'

Khalil flung up a hand. 'Please. Do not defend Aziz to me.' She fell silent and he gazed at her, his mouth thinning. 'Are you so disappointed,' he asked after a moment, 'not to marry Aziz?'

'Only because of what it means for my country. My rule.'

'You are a strong woman, Elena. I think you could stand up to your Council without a husband propping you up.'

She let out a short laugh, not knowing whether to feel offended or flattered. 'Thank you for that vote of confidence, I suppose.'

'I didn't mean it as a criticism. You've shown me with your actions how strong and courageous you are. I think you could face your Council on your own, convince this Markos not to depose you. The vote has to be unanimous, doesn't it?'

'Yes.' She eyed him shrewdly even as she fought a lonely

sweep of desolation. 'Are you trying to make me feel better, or ease your own guilt at having wrecked my marriage plans?'

He looked surprised by the question, or perhaps his own answer. 'Both, I suppose. Although a few days ago I wouldn't have given your plans a single thought.' He shook his head wonderingly, and then his expression hardened once more and he rose from her side. 'I will be busy meeting with various leaders of the local tribes today, but I will see you at the wedding festivities tonight.'

She nodded, still smarting from their conversation, and all Khalil hadn't said. That he didn't feel.

She spent the rest of the day with the women, preparing for the wedding that evening. She helped make bread and stew meat, then when the food was finished and the sun was high in the sky the women headed back down to the oasis to prepare themselves for the festivities.

The bride was a lovely young girl with thick, dark hair, liquid eyes and a nervous smile. Elena watched as the women prepared her for her wedding: a dress of bright blue with rich embroidery on the sleeves and hem, hennaed hands and feet and a veil made of dozens of small copper coins.

What would her own wedding have looked like? she wondered as she watched the women laugh and joke with the young bride. A solemn, private ceremony in one of the reception rooms of the Kadaran palace, no doubt, witnessed by a few of Aziz's staff. Nothing fancy, nothing joyful or exciting.

And the wedding night? She shivered suddenly to think how she would have been giving her body to Aziz, a man she barely knew. Would she have felt for him even an ounce of the desire she felt for Khalil?

Inexorably her mind moved onto the man who always seemed to be in her thoughts. The man everyone here thought was her husband. Wouldn't it be wonderful, she thought suddenly, longingly, to pretend just for one day, for one night, that he was? That she was young and giddy with love, just as this pretty bride was?

What was the harm in that—in a single day of pretending?

Tomorrow she would return to reality. Soon she would be back in Thallia, facing a disapproving Council, forced to tell them her marriage plans had been cancelled. Perhaps facing the end of a monarchy that had lasted for nearly a thousand years—all because she hadn't been strong or smart enough to hold onto her crown.

Yes, one day of pretending sounded wonderful.

And so Elena let herself be carried along once more by the women; she didn't protest when they dressed her in a gown of silvery blue, lined her eyes with kohl, placed copper bangles on both arms and a veil of coins over her face. She understood they wanted to celebrate her recent marriage, just as the young bride was celebrating hers, and she didn't resist.

She wanted to celebrate it too.

The sky was deep indigo and studded with millions of stars when the ceremony began. The entire tribe had assembled and Elena watched, enchanted, as the ceremony played out amidst a riot of colour, music and dance. The women and men sat separately, and although she looked for him she could not find Khalil amidst the men gathered under a tent. She wondered if he would even recognise her in the Bedouin dress, headscarf and veil, wondered what he would think of her like this.

After the ceremony people circulated freely to enjoy food, music and dance. Several giggling women pushed Elena towards a group of men and then she saw him standing there, dressed in a traditional white cotton *thobe* richly embroidered with red and gold.

Khalil seemed to stare right through her and Elena knew

he didn't recognise her. Emboldened by the women who had pushed her forward, or perhaps simply by the desires of her own heart, she walked towards him.

'Greetings, husband,' she said softly. She'd meant to sound teasing but her voice came out earnest instead. Khalil glanced down at her, clearly startled, and then heat filled his eyes and his whole body tensed.

'Elena.'

'What do you think?' She twirled around and her dress flared out, the coins covering the lower part of her face jingling as she moved.

'I think you look lovely.' He placed a hand on her shoulder to stop her in mid-twirl, and drew her closer to him. 'Very lovely indeed. Sometimes something hidden is more alluring than something seen.'

Suddenly she was breathless, dazed by the look of undisguised admiration in his eyes. 'Do you really think so?' she whispered.

'Yes. And now I think the people of the tribe are expecting us to dance.'

'Dance?'

'I know the steps. Follow my lead.' And with one hand on her waist, the other clasped with hers, he led her to the circle of dancers.

The next hour passed in a blur of music and dance, every second one of heightened, almost painful awareness. Khalil's hand in hers, his body next to hers, his gaze fastened to hers, everything in her pulsing with longing. She'd never felt so beautiful or desirable, so heady with a kind of power she'd never, ever experienced before.

When she moved, Khalil's gaze followed her. When she spoke, he leaned forward to listen. She felt as if she were, at this moment, the centre of his universe. And it was the most wonderful feeling in the world.

She never wanted it to end.

But of course it did; the bridal couple was seen off and

people began to trail back to their dwellings. Elena turned to Khalil, uncertainty and hope warring within her. He gazed down at her, his expression inscrutable.

'They have arranged for us to share a tent tonight. I hope you don't mind.'

Mind? No, she didn't mind at all. 'That's…that's all right,' she managed.

Smiling faintly, Khalil threaded his fingers through hers and drew her away from the others…towards the tent they would share.

CHAPTER EIGHT

KHALIL KNEW HE was a little drunk. He hadn't had any alcohol to drink; none had been served. Yet he still felt dazed, almost drugged with possibility. With something deeper and stronger than mere lust, even if part of him wanted to give it that name, make it that simple.

He held the tent flap open for Elena and watched as she moved past him, her Bedouin clothing emphasising the sinuous swing of her hips, her graceful gait. Once in the tent she turned to him and he saw the expectation in her eyes, felt it in himself.

Tonight, to all intents and purposes, they were married. Husband and wife.

'Did you have a good time this evening?' he asked and she nodded.

'Yes... I don't know when I've had a better time, actually.' She let out a little laugh, sounding self-conscious, uncertain. 'I haven't gone to many parties before.'

'Not gone to parties? Not even royal or state functions?'

She shook her head, her grey eyes heartbreakingly wide above her veil. 'I've gone to those, but they weren't...they weren't fun. I could never just be myself. I was always Queen Elena and sometimes it felt like an act.'

'A danger of wearing the crown so young, I suppose. But you should be proud of yourself, Elena, and all you have accomplished.'

He took a step towards her, the need to touch her growing with every moment they spent together. His palms itched and he had to keep himself from reaching for her. 'And were you yourself tonight, Elena? Looking as you do, like a Bedouin girl?'

'Strangely, yes.' She let out another laugh, this one breathy. 'I felt more free tonight than I have in a long time.'

'Free—and yet captive.' He didn't know why he felt the need to remind her of the truth of their situation just then, only that he did. Perhaps he was trying to remind himself to hold onto reality when all he really wanted was to slip the veil from her face and the dress from her body.

'I don't feel like a captive any more, Khalil. I want to be here with you. You might have brought me here, but I'm choosing this now.'

He saw a bold purpose in her eyes now. The innocent, it seemed, had become a seductress. A siren. She walked towards him, lowering the veil of coins away from her face, and placed her hands on his chest. He gazed down at her long, slender fingers, felt them tremble against him. 'Tonight I want to forget everything, Khalil. Everything but you.'

Desire pulsed through him, blurred his brain along with his vision. 'Elena—'

'*Please.*'

He covered her hands with his own; he'd meant to remove them but as soon as he touched her he knew he wouldn't. He knew he needed at least this much, because there wouldn't be much more.

There couldn't be.

'Elena,' he said again, and she shook her head, her hair escaping from underneath her veil, tumbling about her shoulders as dark as a desert night.

'Don't, Khalil,' she whispered. 'Don't say no to me now.'

'Do you even know what you're asking?' he demanded, his voice low, raw and ragged with a desire he couldn't deny.

'Yes, I do.' She met his gaze. 'I'm asking you to make love to me. With me.'

Khalil's breath escaped in a hiss. 'Yes, but you don't know what that means.'

Her eyes flashed sudden fire. 'Don't tell me what I know or don't know, Khalil. I'm perfectly aware of what it means. What I'm asking.'

He arched an eyebrow. 'Are you sure about that, Elena? Because, if I'm not very much mistaken, I believe you're a virgin.'

She flushed but didn't lower her challenging gaze. 'Practical experience isn't required to make an informed choice.'

He almost laughed then, both amused by and admiring of her boldness and courage. His hands tightened on hers as he considered the possibility.

One night… One wonderful, amazing, incredible night…

'It's dangerous,' he began, and she shook her head.

'I know there are ways to prevent a pregnancy, if you don't have any protection.'

Her cheeks had turned fiery and he almost laughed. 'Oh, you do? As it happens, I have protection.'

Surprise made her jaw drop. 'You do?'

'Not,' he continued swiftly, 'because I intended to use it.'

She eyed him sceptically. 'Really?'

'I just like to be prepared.'

She looked uncertain then, even vulnerable. 'Have you had many lovers, then?'

'Not as many as you're thinking, and none in the last year. I've been too busy with other things.' *And none like you*. Untouched. Innocent. Amazing. He couldn't believe he was seriously thinking about taking Elena up on her offer. About making love to her.

'When I said it was dangerous, Elena, I didn't mean an unplanned pregnancy. I was talking about the…the emotional risks.'

She flinched and then recovered her composure. 'I'm aware of the risk, Khalil,' she told him. 'And I'm not under the illusion that this would be anything but one night. I'm not asking for more from you.'

'I know that.'

'Then what's the problem?' He just shook his head, both torn and tempted. Her smile turned flirtatious, even sultry. 'I suppose I'll just have to seduce you.'

Surprise flared deep inside him, along with an almost unbearable arousal. 'I don't think that's a good idea,' he managed. He knew she wouldn't have to do much and he would cave completely. He would take her in his arms and lose himself in her kiss, in her body.

He took a defensive step backwards and Elena's mouth curved in the kind of wicked little smile he hadn't known she was capable of.

'Scared, Khalil?'

'Tempted, Elena. And I'd rather not be.'

'Are you sure about that?' Slowly she lifted her arms, the wide sleeves of her dress falling back to reveal her slender wrists, and began to unwind her headscarf. Her kohl-lined eyes were wide and dark as she slowly unwrapped the garment, and Khalil simply watched, entranced by the utterly feminine and sensual act of undressing.

He heard his breath come out in something close to a pant as she dropped the headscarf and then shrugged out of her dress.

Underneath she wore only a thin chemise of bleached cotton, the material nearly transparent. He could see the temptingly round fullness of her breasts, the shadow between her thighs. He stifled a groan.

She moved closer, her eyes full of an ancient feminine power. She knew how she affected him and it made her bold.

It made her irresistible.

Her hands slid up his chest and he knew she could feel

how his heart was racing. His mind had stalled at the sight of her and it now kicked desperately into gear.

'I really don't think this is a good idea, Elena.'

'Too bad, then, that I do.' She stood on her tiptoes and brushed a butterfly kiss across his mouth. 'That's only the second kiss I've ever had,' she whispered against his lips. 'The first was two nights ago, when you held me on your lap.'

He closed his eyes. He was the only man who had ever kissed her? Didn't she realise how much she was giving him, offering him freely? Didn't she know how hurt she might be afterwards? No matter what she said or promised now, she was young. Inexperienced. Innocent.

He forced his eyes open, wrapped his hands around hers and attempted to draw them away from him. 'I don't want to hurt you, Elena.'

'You won't.'

'You don't know that. You *can't* know that, because you've never done this before.'

'And when am I going to get a chance to do it, Khalil?' she asked, her honest gaze clashing with his. 'I was going to give myself to a man I barely knew for the sake of my country. That possibility has been taken away from me now. You've taken it away from me, and I think it's only fair you offer me something in return. You owe me a wedding night.'

He let out a ragged laugh. 'I never thought of it that way.'

'Think of it that way now,' she said, and kissed him again. Her lips were soft, warm and open and her breasts brushed his chest. Khalil's arms came around her without him having made a conscious decision to embrace her, yet suddenly he was. He pulled her closer, fitting her softness against his body, pressing against her, craving the contact. And as her lips parted and she innocently, instinctively deepened the kiss, he knew he was lost.

This was what she wanted. Needed. Elena wound her arms around Khalil's neck as he took over her tentative kiss and made it his own. Made it theirs. His tongue slid into her mouth, exploring its contours and causing shivers of amazed pleasure to ripple through her. She had never known a kiss could be so consuming. So...*much*.

He slid one hand from her shoulder to cup her breast, his palm warm and sure. Elena shuddered under his touch. The intensity of her pleasure was almost painful, and yet achingly exquisite. And, while this was so much more than she'd ever felt or experienced before, it still wasn't enough. She felt an ache deep inside for more and she acted on it.

She pushed the *thobe* from his shoulders, and wordlessly Khalil shrugged out of it; the loose linen shirt and trousers he wore underneath followed. He was completely naked and utterly beautiful, long, lean, lithe and yet incredibly powerful, his body rippling with muscle. Now more than ever he reminded her of a panther, beautiful, awe-inspiring and just a little bit scary.

This was scary. Wonderful, exciting, new—and scary. She took a deep breath and waited for him to make the next move because she wasn't sure what it should be.

He lifted the hem of her chemise and she raised her arms so he could take it off her. She wore nothing underneath and, as his gaze roved over her nakedness, she felt a twinge of embarrassment, extinguished when he ran a gentle hand from her shoulder to thigh.

'You are so beautiful, Elena.'

'You are too,' she whispered and he laughed softly and tugged on her hand, leading her towards the bed.

He lay down on the soft covers and drew her down next to him so they were facing each other. Elena's breath was already coming in short gasps; her senses were on overload simply by lying next to Khalil, his naked body so close to hers. His chest rippled with muscle and his belly was taut and flat. Her gaze dipped lower and then moved up again;

she might have been talking a big game but she was still inexperienced. Still a little nervous.

Khalil took her hand and placed it on his bare chest. 'We can stop,' he said quietly; it amazed her how he always seemed to know what she was thinking, feeling. 'We can always stop.'

'I don't want to stop,' she told him with a shaky laugh. 'That doesn't mean I'm not going to be a little nervous, though.'

'Understandable,' he murmured, and kissed her again, a kiss that was slow and soft and wonderful. A kiss that banished any lingering fears or feelings of nervousness. A kiss that felt like a promise, although of what Elena couldn't say.

He slid his hand down her body, rested it on the flat of her tummy, waited. Everything in Elena quivered with anticipation. She wanted him to touch her…everywhere.

Still kissing her, he moved his hand lower. He waited again for the acceptance that she gave, his fingers brushing between her thighs, everything in her straining and yearning for even more.

And as he touched her with such wonderful, knowing expertise she realised she wanted to touch him too. She felt a new boldness come over her, a certainty to take what she wanted—and give him what he wanted. She smoothed her hands over his chest, slid her fingers across the ridged muscles of his abdomen. She wrapped them around the length of his arousal, causing his breath to come out in a hiss of pleasure which increased her own and made her bolder still.

With each caress the pressure in her built, a desperate need demanding satisfaction. And even she, in her innocence and inexperience, knew how it would finally be satisfied.

She rolled onto her back as he put on the condom and then positioned himself over her, braced on his forearms, his breath coming out in a ragged pant as he waited. 'Are you sure…?'

'Of course I'm sure, Khalil,' she half-laughed, half-sobbed, because by then she was more than sure. She was ready.

And then he entered her, slowly, the sensation so strange and yet so right at the same time. He went deeper, and with an instinct she hadn't known she possessed she arched her hips upwards and wrapped her legs around his waist. Pulled him deeper into herself.

'Okay?' he muttered and she almost laughed.

'Yes. Yes. More than okay.' And she was. She felt powerful in that moment, as well as loved. As if, with Khalil, she could do anything. She could be the person she was meant to be. She'd thought trusting someone, loving someone, made you weak, left you open and vulnerable to hurt. But right now she felt utterly strong. Completely whole.

And then he started to move, and the friction of his body inside hers increased that ache of pleasure deep within her, a sensation that built to such strength she felt as if it would explode from her, as if she would fly from the force of it, soaring high above the little camp, above everything.

And then it happened, everything in her peaking in an explosion of pleasure: she cried out, one long, ragged note, and fell back against the pillows, her body still wrapped around Khalil's, his head buried in the curve of her shoulder.

Neither of them spoke for several long minutes; Elena could feel the thud of Khalil's heart against her own, both of them racing. She stared up at the ceiling of the tent and wondered how she'd gone as long as she had without experiencing such incredible intimacy. Feeling such an amazing sense of rightness and power.

Slowly Khalil moved off her. He lay on his back, staring up at the ceiling, and Elena felt the first pinprick of uncertainty. Suddenly he seemed remote.

'I didn't hurt you,' he said, not quite a question, and she shook her head.

'No.'

'Good.' He rose then, magnificent in his nakedness, and went to dress.

'Khalil…' She rose up onto her elbows. 'Don't.'

'Don't what?'

'You owe me a wedding night, not a wedding hour,' she told him, trying to sound teasing even though nerves leapt in her belly and fluttered in her throat. 'Come back to bed.'

He stared at her for an endless moment, his *thobe* clenched in one hand, and Elena thought he would refuse—walk out of the tent and leave her alone with nothing but memories and regret. Then with a slight shrug he dropped the garment. He returned to the bed, sitting on its edge, away from her. She saw several faded white scars crisscrossing his back, and wondered at them. Now, she knew, was not the time to ask.

'I don't want to hurt you, Elena,' he said quietly. 'And I don't mean physically.'

She swallowed hard. 'I know you don't.'

He gave a slight shake of his head. 'The closer we become, *seem*…'

Seem. Because tonight's intimacy wasn't real, at least not for him. 'I understand, Khalil,' she told him. 'You don't have to warn me again. Tonight is a fantasy. Tomorrow it ends. Trust me, I get that. I accept it.'

He let out a weary sigh and gently she laid a hand on his shoulder, her fingers curling around warm skin, and pulled him back towards her. After a second's resistance, he came, lying next to her, folding her into his arms and then hauling her against his chest.

It felt like the only place she'd ever really belonged.

For tonight.

Neither of them spoke for several long minutes; Khalil stroked her hair and Elena rested one hand on his chest, perfectly content.

Almost.

The knowledge that this was only temporary, only tonight, ate away at her happiness, poked holes in this moment's peace. She tried to banish that knowledge; she wanted to dwell only in the fantasy now.

Closing her eyes, she imagined that they were in fact wed, that the ceremony tonight had been theirs. That they lay here as husband and wife, utterly in love with each other.

As she embroidered each detail onto the cloth of her imagination, she knew she was being foolish. Understood that envisioning such a thing, such a life, even if only as a fantasy, was dangerous.

Khalil didn't want a relationship, a loving relationship, and she didn't either. At least, she shouldn't. She'd never wanted it before. She'd chosen not to look for love, not to trust someone with her heart, her life. She'd done it once before—not romantically, but the betrayal had still wounded her deeply. Had made her doubt not just other people but herself.

How could she have trusted someone who had used her so spectacularly?

And how could she ever risk herself to trust again?

No, she was better off without love or romance. Keeping it as a fantasy, a single night.

And maybe, if she kept telling herself that, she'd believe it.

'What are you thinking about, Elena?' Khalil asked, his voice a quiet rumble in his chest.

'Nothing—'

'Not nothing,' he interjected quietly. 'You've gone all tense.'

And she realised she had; she was lying stiff in his arms, her hand curled against his chest. Gently he reached up and flattened her fist, smoothing her fingers out before resting his hand on top of hers. 'What were you thinking about?' he asked again.

She sighed. 'Just…some memories.'

'The same memories that give you nightmares?'

'No. Different ones.'

'Not good ones, though.'

'No.' She let out a little sigh. 'Not particularly.'

'I'm sorry,' he said after a moment, and somehow that felt like exactly the right thing to say.

'So am I. But I don't want to think about bad memories tonight, Khalil. I want to be happy. Just for tonight.'

He squeezed her hand lightly. 'I won't stop you.'

'I know, but…' She wanted more than his acquiescence; she wanted his participation. 'Can we—can we pretend?' she asked, her voice quavering slightly with nervousness. 'Can we pretend, just for tonight, that we're…that we're in love?' She felt his body tense underneath her hand and she hurried to explain. 'I know we're not. I don't want us to be, not for real. I don't want to love someone like that.' Khalil remained ominously silent, so she continued stiltedly, 'I just want to feel like I do for one night. To forget everything else and just enjoy feelings I can't afford to have in real life.' She sounded ridiculous, Elena realised. What was she really asking? For him to *pretend* to love her?

How absurd. How pathetic.

And Khalil still hadn't said anything.

'Maybe it's a stupid idea,' Elena muttered. Inwardly she cringed at the whole ridiculous proposition she'd put before him. 'I didn't mean… You don't have to worry that I'll suddenly…' Her throat tightened and she was about to force herself to go on, to reassure him that she wouldn't fall in love with him or start expecting emotions and commitments from him simply because they'd had sex, but then Khalil spoke first.

'For one night,' he said slowly. 'I think I can manage that…my darling.'

Surprise gave way to mirth and even joy, and she let out

a bubble of laughter, shaking her head. 'Now, that rolled off the tongue quite nicely,' she teased.

'Did it not, dearest?' He raised his eyebrows, turning to her with an enquiring smile. 'What shall I call you, then, essence of sweetness?'

She turned her head towards the pillow to muffle her laughter. '*Essence of sweetness?* Where do you come up with that stuff?'

'It comes naturally, my dewy petal,' he purred. 'Can't you tell?'

Tears of laughter started in her eyes. Her stomach ached. And she felt the biggest, sloppiest grin spreading over her face. 'Sorry, but I can't tell.'

Khalil rose on his arms above her, a wicked smile curving his mouth and glinting in his eyes. 'What a dilemma,' he answered softly. 'Since I don't seem able to tell you how I love you, then perhaps I should show you.'

And then Elena's laughter stopped abruptly as he did precisely that—showing her with his mouth, his hands and body. And he showed her very well indeed.

CHAPTER NINE

KHALIL AWAKENED TO sunlight streaming into their tent and Elena's hair spread over his chest. He'd slept the whole night with his arms around her, his body entwined with hers, and it had felt good.

Unbearably good.

What on earth had possessed him to participate in her little game? Pretend to be in *love?* And, never mind the danger involved in that all too enjoyable charade, what about the fact that he'd slept with her at all? That he'd taken her virginity? No matter what she'd assured him about understanding the emotional risks, he knew it was dangerous. Dangerous for her, and even dangerous for him, because already he wanted her again—and not just in bed.

In his life.

And there was no place for Queen Elena of Thallia in his life.

The next few days and weeks were crucial to his campaign to retake the throne that was rightfully his. He couldn't waste a moment's energy or thought on anything but his goal, a goal he'd nourished and cherished since he'd been seven years old and had been dropped into the desert like a dog no one wanted. Treated like one too, kicked and beaten and abused.

And, in any case, he didn't do love. He didn't know how. Trusting another person with *anything,* much less his heart—dried-up, useless organ that it was—was next to impossible for him. He wanted to trust people, men like Assad who had sworn their loyalty to him, but he still always felt that prickle of wary suspicion between his shoulder blades. He was still, always, waiting for the sudden slap, the knife in the back. The betrayal.

When you lived your life like that, love had no place in it. Relationships had no place, save for expediency.

And as for Elena? He glanced down at her, her face softened in sleep, her dark, lush lashes feathering her cheeks. Her lips were slightly pursed, one hand flung up by her head. Despite his mental list of reasons to walk away right now, desire stirred insistently. He knew just how he could wake her up…

Swearing under his breath, Khalil extracted himself from Elena's embrace and rolled from the bed. He heard her stir behind him, but he was already yanking on his clothes, his back determinedly to her.

A serving maid entered, blushing, with a pitcher of hot water and inwardly Khalil swore again. The news of their night together would spread throughout the whole tribe. They would know he had consummated a union that he intended to reject shortly.

And his plan to explain later why he'd been travelling alone with Elena would no longer work. He'd acted dishonourably and the tribe would know it. When they found out he and Elena weren't married, they would feel both betrayed and angry, and how could he blame them?

It was a fiasco, and all because he'd wanted her so damn much. How could he have been so weak?

'Khalil…?'

He turned to see her sitting up in bed, her dark hair tumbling wildly about her shoulders, her hooded grey eyes sleepy but with a wariness already stealing into them.

'We need to get moving,' he said brusquely. 'Assad is coming with a vehicle this morning. He'll take us to a new camp and then we'll move onto Siyad. You'll be back in Thallia this time tomorrow, I hope.'

She looked away, hiding her face, but he still felt the hurt he knew he'd caused her. Damn it, he'd *warned* her about this. He couldn't blame Elena, though. He could only blame himself. He'd known she was a virgin, inexperienced and innocent. She was bound to read more into their night together, even if she'd said she wouldn't.

Hell, he'd read more into it. Felt more than he was comfortable with.

And now he had no idea what to do, how to make things right: with Elena; with the tribe; with this country of his that teetered on the brink of civil war, made worse by his own foolish choices.

What an unholy mess.

After Khalil had left the tent Elena rose slowly from the bed and reached for the Bedouin-style dress he'd stripped from her body the night before.

Had it only been the night before? It felt like a lifetime ago. Felt like a different life, one where she'd known pleasure, joy and love.

It was only pretend, you idiot.

Sighing, she slipped on the chemise, only to see her Western clothes lying neatly folded by the pitcher of water. She took off the chemise and washed quickly, scrubbing the scent of Khalil from her body, before putting on the clothes she'd come here in.

Time to return to reality.

By the time she'd eaten breakfast—with the other women, Khalil not in sight—some of her equilibrium had been restored, along with her determination.

She'd had setbacks before, been hurt before. And this time she had no one to blame but herself. Khalil had been honest with her, unlike Paulo had been. He'd told her what she could and couldn't expect, and he'd been true to his word. She could not fault him.

And so she wouldn't. She'd had her night, her fantasy, and she'd treasure it—but she wouldn't let it consume or control her. Life had to go on and, with the end of her captivity looming ever nearer, she needed to think about her return to Thallia.

Just the thought made her feel as if she'd swallowed a stone.

After breakfast Khalil came for her, his *thobe* billowing out behind him, the set of his face exceptionally grim. Even scowling he was handsome, with the dark slashes of his eyebrows and those full, sculpted lips. His eyes seemed to glow fire.

'Are you ready? We should leave as soon as possible.'

Elena rose from where she'd been sitting by the fire and brushed the crumbs from her lap. 'I'm ready now.'

Nodding, Khalil turned away, and wordlessly Elena followed him. Assad was waiting by an SUV with blacked-out windows. Elena slid inside, fighting a weird sense of déjà vu. She'd been driven in a car like this when she'd first been captured. Now she was being driven to a freedom she wasn't sure she wanted.

They rode through the unending desert, Assad driving while Khalil and Elena sat in the back, not speaking, not touching.

Despite the ache Khalil's stony silence caused her, Elena forced herself to think practically. In two days she would, God willing, be back in Thallia. What would Andreas Markos have done in her absence? Would he have heard of her abduction, or would Aziz have managed to keep it secret?

She'd only been in the desert for a handful of days, even if it had felt like a lifetime. Perhaps Markos and the rest of her Council weren't yet aware of what had happened.

'Have you heard any news?' she asked Khalil abruptly,

and he turned, eyebrows raised. 'Has Aziz admitted that I'm missing? Does my Council know?'

'Aziz has admitted nothing. I doubt your Council is aware of events.'

'But how has he explained—?'

'He hasn't. He hired someone to pretend to be you and it seems everyone, including your Council, has believed it.'

Shock left her speechless for a moment. 'He did? But—'

'They appeared on the palace balcony two days ago. From a distance the woman fooled the people, or so it would seem. That's all I know.' He arched an eyebrow. 'Your Council wasn't expecting to hear from you, I presume?'

'Not until I returned.' She'd been meant to be on her honeymoon. 'You should have told me,' Elena said and Khalil eyed her coolly.

'What purpose would it have served?'

'It just would have been good to know.' She stared out of the window, tried to sift through her tangled feelings. She wasn't exactly surprised that Aziz had come up with an alternative plan; she'd suggested as much to Khalil. She wasn't hurt by his actions either. But she felt…something and with a jolt she realised it *was* hurt—not for what Aziz had done, but for what Khalil hadn't. Not telling her had been a tactical move, a way of treating her like a political pawn rather than a—what?

Just what was she to him now?

Nothing, obviously. She closed her eyes and thought of him covering her with kisses last night, both of them laughing. *It was pretend. You knew that.*

But it still hurt now.

'I'll be able to tell you more when we return to camp,' Khalil said. He drummed his fingers against the window, clearly restless. 'What will you do when you return to Thallia?' he asked. Elena opened her eyes.

'Do you really care?'

'I'm asking the question.'

'And the answer is, I don't know. It depends what state my country is in. My government.'

'Your Head of Council won't have had time to call a vote to abolish the monarchy.'

'No, but he will as soon as he can.'

'You could marry someone else in the meantime.'

'Suitable husbands are a little thin on the ground.'

'Are they?' He turned back to the window, frowning deeply. Elena had no idea what he was thinking. 'Just what was your arrangement with Aziz?' he asked, still staring out of the window.

'I told you.'

'I mean in practical terms.'

Bewildered, she almost asked him why he wanted to know. Why he cared. Then, with a mental shrug, she answered, 'It was a matter of convenience for both of us. We'd split our time between Thallia and Kadar, rule independently.'

'And that pleased your Council?'

'My Council was not aware of all the terms of the marriage. They probably assumed I'd be more under Aziz's influence.'

'And they didn't mind a stranger helping to rule their country?'

'He's royal in his own right, and as I explained they're traditional. They want me under a man's influence.'

Khalil nodded slowly, his forehead knitted in thought. 'And what about heirs?'

A blush touched her cheeks. 'Why are we talking about this, exactly?'

'I'm curious.'

'And you want me to satisfy your curiosity?' Her temper flared. 'What for, Khalil? None of it is going to happen anyway, and in any case it has nothing to do with you.'

He turned to her with a granite stare. 'Humour me.'

Her breath came out in a rush. 'We planned for two children, an heir for each of our kingdoms.'

'And where would these children have been raised?'

'Initially they would stay with me, and when they were older they would split their time between the two countries.' She looked away, uncomfortably aware of how cold and clinical it sounded. 'I know it's hardly an ideal solution, but we were both desperate.'

'I realise that.'

'Like I said, it doesn't matter anyway.'

'But you still feel you need a husband.'

She sighed and leaned her head back against the seat, closing her eyes once more. 'I do, but maybe you're right. Maybe I can face my Council on my own, convince them not to call the vote.'

'It's a risk.'

She opened her eyes. 'You don't sound nearly as encouraging as you did before.'

He shrugged. 'You have to choose for yourself.'

'Seeing as there's nothing to choose, as I have no prospective husband, this whole conversation seems pointless.'

'Maybe,' Khalil allowed, and turned back to the window. 'Maybe not.'

He could marry her. The thought made everything in him rear up in shocked panic. Marriage had never been on his agenda. Yet ever since he'd seen that serving girl this morning, and realised the repercussions of his night with Elena, the thought had been rattling around in his brain like a coin in a box.

He could marry her—marry the woman who was intended as the Sheikh of Kadar's wife. It would help strengthen his claim, stabilise his throne, and it would give Elena what she wanted too.

Why not?

Because it's dangerous. Because the emotional risks you warned her about apply to you too.

Because you care about her already.

Elena had spoken of a cold, convenient union, but would it be like that if he was her husband? Would he be able to keep himself from caring for, even loving, her?

Did he even want to?

His mind spun and seethed. He felt the clash of his own desires, the need to protect himself and the urge to be with her—care for her.

And did Elena even care for him? Just what kind of marriage would she want them to have?

Once back at the camp—which to Elena looked like just another huddle of tents, horses, cars and camels amidst the dunes and black rocks—Khalil strode away and Leila met Elena and brought her to her private tent.

'A bath, perhaps,' she murmured and Elena thanked her, nodding wearily. She felt overwhelmed by every aspect of life at the moment: the end of things here, her responsibilities in Thallia, her non-relationship with Khalil.

A quarter of an hour later she watched as two men filled the copper tub with steaming water. Leila scattered it with rose petals and brought a thick towel and some lovely smelling soap, and Elena's throat suddenly went tight with emotion.

'Thank you. This is so kind…'

'It is nothing, Your Highness. You could use a little pampering, I think.'

The older woman's sympathy was almost her undoing. Elena nodded, swallowing past the tightness in her throat as Leila quietly left.

As she soaked in the tub Elena's thoughts returned relentlessly to Thallia and matters of state. She had no husband. She could explain why and, since it looked as if

Khalil would become Sheikh, she thought her Council would accept it.

But in a few weeks' time, if she were still single, Markos would call for the vote to abolish the monarchy. Somehow she had to convince him not to call it, or at least convince her Council not to vote against her.

Could she do it on her own? Did she dare risk her crown in such a way? Khalil believed in her, perhaps more than she believed in herself. Just remembering the warmth of his smile, the confidence she'd seen in his eyes, made her ache.

No, she couldn't risk it. A royal wedding and a devoted husband were what had been going to save her, no matter what Khalil said about her being strong enough to face her Council alone. He didn't know what she was up against. Didn't understand what she'd been through.

Sighing, Elena leaned her head back against the tub. The only way to avoid such a disaster would be to prove Markos wrong—to return with a husband.

Too bad that was impossible.

Unless she married Khalil.

Elena smiled mirthlessly as she imagined Khalil's horrified reaction to such an idea. He would never agree to marry her. He'd been appalled by the possibility that she might harbour any tender feelings for him. He'd sounded contemptuous of her arrangement with Aziz.

Elena sat up suddenly, water sloshing over the sides of the tub. Marrying her could potentially be beneficial for Khalil. She'd seen the approval of the Bedouin they'd been with, how they'd liked seeing him with his bride.

And since he'd already acted as if they were married…

Could it be possible? Did she even dare suggest a thing? The potential rejection and humiliation she faced made her flinch.

Then, in a sudden, painful rush of memory, Elena recalled her father throwing himself over her, saving her life from the explosions and gunfire around them. Sacrificing himself…for Thallia. For the monarchy.

How could she not do whatever it took to ensure her reign?

An hour later she was dressed in another outfit Leila had brought her, a simple dress of rose-coloured cotton. She twisted her hair up in a chignon and wished she had some make-up or jewellery to make her feel more prepared. She was going to talk to Khalil. Beard the lion in his den.

Taking a deep breath, Elena square her shoulders and exited the tent. Two guards immediately moved in front of her, blocking her way.

Fury surged through her, shocking her with its intensity. 'Really?' she asked them. 'After everything, you still think I'm going to run off into the desert?'

They stared back at her blandly. 'Do you want for something, Your Highness?'

A husband. She took another deep breath. 'I would like to speak to Khalil.'

'He is not—'

'Available? Well, make him available. I need to speak to him, and it's important.'

Leila came hurrying over, her face creased with concern. 'Your Highness? Is something wrong?'

'I'd like to speak to Khalil,' Elena stated. Her voice wobbled and, furious with herself, she bit her lip. Hard. 'Do you know where he is, Leila?' she asked, and thankfully this time her voice was steady.

Leila gazed at her, a certain sorrowful knowledge in her eyes, and Elena had the sudden, awful suspicion that Leila knew she and Khalil had slept together.

'Yes, I know where he is,' she said quietly. She spoke in Arabic to the two guards, but her voice was too low for Elena to make anything out. Then she turned back to her and said, 'Come with me.'

Elena went. Leila led her to a tent on the opposite side of the camp, pausing outside the entrance to turn back to her.

'Khalil has been through much, Your Highness,' she said quietly. 'Whatever has happened between the two of you, please remember that.'

So Leila had definitely guessed, then. Elena forced the realisation away and met her gaze squarely. 'I just want to talk to him, Leila.'

'I know.' The older woman smiled sadly. 'But I can tell you are hurting, and I am sorry for it. Khalil is hurting too.'

Khalil hurting? *I don't think so.* But Elena was still considering Leila's words as she stepped into the tent and looked upon Khalil.

He was seated at a folding table, his dark head bent as he scrawled something on a piece of paper. He didn't look up, just lifted one hand, signalling her to wait.

'One moment, Assad, please.'

'It's not Assad.'

Khalil glanced up swiftly then, his gaze narrowing as it rested on Elena. She stared back, levelly, she hoped, but after a taut few seconds she knew she was glaring.

'Elena.'

'*Khalil.*' She mimicked his even tone, slightly sneering it. Oops. Not the way she'd wanted to start this business-like meeting, but then Leila was right. She *was* hurting, even if she didn't want to be.

He sat back, resting his arms lightly on the sides of his chair. 'Is there something you need?'

'You had said you would look at the news,' Elena reminded him. 'Find out if people know what has happened.'

'So I did. I haven't seen anything so far. Aziz is keeping quiet.'

'And how will you return me to Thallia?' she asked coolly. 'Royal jet? Economy class? Or will you roll me up in a carpet like Cleopatra and then unroll me in the throne room of the Thallian palace?'

'An interesting possibility.' His gaze rested on her, assessing, penetrating. 'Why are you so angry, Elena?'

'I'm not angry.'

'You sound angry.'

'I'm frustrated. There's a difference.'

'Very well, then. Why are you frustrated?'

'Because I came to Kadar with a plan to save my throne and I no longer have one.'

'You mean marriage.'

'Yes.'

His gaze narrowed. 'And what would you like me to do about it?'

'I'm glad you asked.' Elena took a deep breath, tried to smile as she met his narrowed gaze. 'I'd like you to marry me.'

CHAPTER TEN

SHE'D BEATEN HIM to it, Khalil thought bemusedly, even as an elemental panic clawed at his insides. He'd been considering marriage to Elena as a solution to both of their problems since this morning. Yet looking at her now, seeing the hope and determination blazing in her eyes, everything in him resisted. There had to be another solution.

Slowly he shook his head. 'That's impossible, Elena.'

'Why is it impossible?' she demanded.

'Because I have no wish or reason to marry you, Elena.' Better to be brutal. Nip it in the bud, if he could. 'You may be desperate, but I am not.'

She flinched, but only slightly. 'Are you sure about that, Khalil?'

'Quite sure. You asked for a wedding night, Elena, not a marriage.'

'Well, now I'm asking for a marriage.'

'And I'm telling you the answer is no.' He rose from his chair, fought the panic that was crashing over him in tidal waves. 'This discussion is over.'

She raised her eyebrows, a small smile playing about her mouth. A mouth he'd kissed. Tasted. He forced his gaze upwards but her eyes just reminded him of how they'd been filled with need and joy when he'd slid inside her. Her hair reminded him of how soft and silky it had felt spread across his chest. Everything about her was dangerous, every memory a minefield of emotion.

'You don't even want to think about it?' she challenged and he folded his arms.

'I do not.'

'You almost sound scared, Khalil,' she taunted, and fury pulsed through him because he knew she was right. Talking about marriage scared the hell out of him, because he was afraid it wouldn't be the cold, convenient arrangement she'd intended to have with Aziz. She'd want more. *He* would.

And that was far, far too dangerous.

'It's simply not an option,' he told her shortly.

'Even though you've already told people we're married?'

He felt his jaw bunch, his teeth grit. 'I didn't tell anyone.'

'Semantics, Khalil. The result was the same. And, no matter what you tell yourself or me, there will still be re-percussions for you.'

'I'm perfectly aware of that, Elena.' He heard a patron-ising note enter his voice and knew it was the lowest form of self-defence. Everything she was saying was true, yet still he fought it. 'As I told you before, by the time people learn the truth I will be established in Siyad as Sheikh.'

'And that's how you want to start your rule? Based on a lie?'

He pressed his lips together, forced the anger back. 'Not particularly, but events dictated it be thus. I will deal with the consequences as best as I can.' All because of his own stupid weakness concerning this woman.

'And what if your people decide you might be lying about other things? What if they assume you lied about your parentage and Aziz is the true heir?'

Just like his father had lied. He would be no better, and the realisation made him sick with both shame and fury. 'Are you trying to argue your way into a marriage the way you argued your way into my bed?' he demanded, and she flinched then, her face crumpling a little before she quickly looked away. Khalil swore softly. 'Elena,' he said quietly, 'I understand you feel you need a husband. But I am not that man.'

He couldn't be.

'It makes sense,' she whispered. She still wouldn't look at him and the fury left him in a weary rush. He wanted to pull her into his arms. Kiss her sadness away.

But he couldn't marry her. He couldn't open himself up to that weakness, that risk, that *pain*.

'I can see how it might make sense to you,' he said carefully. 'You need a convenient husband.'

'And you need a convenient wife.' She swung around to face him with a challenging stare. 'Your people want you to marry. We saw that when we were with them. They think you're married to me already! One day you'll need an heir—'

'One day.' Khalil cut her off swiftly. 'Not yet.'

'I won't ask anything of you that you wouldn't want to give,' Elena continued doggedly. 'I won't fall in love with you, or demand your time or attention. We can come to an arrangement, like I had with Aziz—'

'Don't mention his name,' Khalil said, his voice coming out like the crack of a whip. Elena's eyes widened; she was startled, and so was he.

Where was all this emotion coming from? This anger and...*hurt*? Because the thought of her with Aziz made his blood boil and his stomach churn. He couldn't bear to think of her with anyone else, not even a man he knew she didn't love, barely knew.

They stared at each other, the very air seeming to spark with the electric charge that pulsed between them: anger and attraction. Desire and frustration.

'I won't, then,' Elena said quietly. 'But you could at least think of it, Khalil. You'll have to marry some day. Why not me? Unless...' She paused, nibbling her lip. 'Unless you're holding out for love.'

'I am not.'

'Well, then.'

He just shook his head, unwilling to articulate just why he was rejecting her proposal out of hand. He couldn't admit to her that he was actually *scared*. 'What about you? You're not interested in love?'

She hesitated, and he saw the truth in her eyes. She was. She wouldn't admit it to him, but she was. 'I can't afford to be interested in love.'

'You might decide one day you want someone who loves you,' he pointed out, trying to sound reasonable when in fact he felt incredibly, insanely jealous at the thought of another man loving her. *Touching* her.

'I won't,' she told him. 'I won't let myself.'

'Even if you wanted to?'

'Are you worried I'm going to fall in love with you, Khalil?'

No—he was terrified that he was already in love with her. Khalil spun around. 'Put like that, it sounds arrogant.'

'I'll try to keep myself from it.' She spoke lightly, but he had a feeling she was serious. She didn't want to fall in love with him, and why should she? He would only hurt her. He wouldn't love her back.

Except maybe you already do.

'We've both been hurt before,' Elena said after a moment. 'I know that. Neither of us wants that kind of pain again, which is why an arrangement such as the one I'm suggesting makes so much sense.'

It did. He knew it did. He shouldn't be fighting it. He should be agreeing with her, coolly discussing the arrangements.

Instead he stood there, silent and struggling.

Elena didn't want his love, wouldn't make emotional demands. In that regard, she would make the perfect wife.

And yet looking at her now he saw the welter of hope and sadness in her eyes. Felt it in himself. And he knew that no matter how they spun it, no matter what they agreed on, marriage to Elena would be dangerous. Because, even if some contrary part of him actually longed for the things he said he couldn't do, didn't want—love, intimacy, trust, all of it—the rest of him knew better. Knew that going down that road, allowing himself to feel, yearn and ache, was bad, bad news.

No matter how practical Elena's suggestion might be, he couldn't take it.

'I'm sorry, Elena,' he said. 'But I won't marry you. I can't.'

She stared at him for a moment, her wide, grey eyes dark with sadness, and then turning darker still with acceptance. Slowly she nodded.

'Very well,' she said, and without another word she turned and left the tent.

Khalil stared at the empty space she'd left, his mind spinning, his heart aching, hating that already he felt so bereft.

It had been worth a shot, Elena told herself as she walked back to her tent, escorted by the same men who guarded her. They didn't speak and neither did she, because she knew she wouldn't be able to manage a word. Her throat ached and she was afraid that if she so much as opened her mouth she'd burst into tears.

Back in her tent she sat on her bed, blinking hard to contain all the pain and hurt she felt. Then suddenly, almost angrily, she wondered why she bothered. Why not have a good cry? Let it all out? No one was here to hear her or think her weak or stupid or far too feminine.

She lay down on her bed, drew her knees up to her chest and swallowed hard. Crying—letting herself cry—was so hard. She'd kept everything in for so long because she'd had to. Men like Markos were always looking for chinks in her armour, ways to weaken her authority. Shedding a single tear would have been just handing them ammunition. The only time she ever cried was when she had nightmares.

In Khalil's arms.

She hadn't consciously, deliberately accessed that hidden, vulnerable part of herself for years, and it was hard to reach it now, even when she wanted to. Sort of.

She took a shuddering breath and clutched her knees harder, closed her eyes and felt the pressure build in her chest.

Finally that first tear fell, trickling onto her cheek. She dashed it away instinctively, but another came, and another, and then she really was crying. Her shoulders shaking, the tears streamed as ragged sobs tore from her throat. She pressed her hot face into the pillow and let all the misery out.

It was not just sadness about her wrecked wedding, or Khalil, but about so much more: the needless deaths of her parents and the fact that she hadn't been able to grieve for them as she should have. Her broken relationship with Paulo, her shattered trust. The four lonely years she'd endured as Queen, working hard for the country she loved, suffering Markos's and other councillors' sneers and slights, trying desperately to hold onto the one thing her parents wanted her to keep.

And yes, she realised as she sobbed, she was crying about Khalil. He'd helped her in so many ways, opened her up, allowed her to feel and trust again. She'd miss him more than she wanted to admit even to herself. More than he'd ever want to know.

Khalil turned back to the reports he'd been studying, reports detailing Kadar's response to Aziz, polls that confirmed outside of Siyad he was not a popular choice as Sheikh. It was news that should have encouraged him, but he only felt restless and dissatisfied—and it was all because of Elena. Or, really, all because of him and his reaction to her and her proposal.

He should have said yes. He should have been strong and cold and ruthless enough to agree to a marriage that would stabilise his country, strengthen his claim. Instead he'd let his emotions rule him. His fear had won out, and the realisation filled him with self-fury.

'Your Highness?'

Khalil waved Assad forward, glad to think about something else. 'You have news, Assad?'

Assad nodded, his face as stony and sombre as always. Khalil had met him eight years ago, when he'd joined the French Foreign Legion. They'd fought together, laughed together and saved each other's lives on more than one occasion. And, when the time had been right for Khalil to return to Kadar, Assad had made it possible. He'd gathered support, guarded his back.

None of this would have been possible without Assad, yet Khalil still didn't trust him. But that was his fault, not his friend's.

'Is something the matter?' he asked and Assad gave one terse nod.

'Aziz has married.'

Khalil stilled, everything inside him going cold. He'd always known this was a risk, yet he was still surprised. 'Married? How? Who?'

'We're not sure. Intelligence suggests someone on his staff, a housekeeper or some such.'

'He married his housekeeper?' *Poor Elena.* No matter what she had or hadn't felt for Aziz, it would still be a blow. And with a jolt Khalil realised he shouldn't even be thinking about Elena; he should be thinking about his rule.

Aziz had fulfilled the terms of his father's will. He would be Sheikh.

And Khalil wouldn't.

Abruptly he rose from his chair, stalked to the other

side of the tent. Emotion poured through him in a scalding wave, emotion he would never have let himself feel a week ago. Before Elena.

She'd accessed that hidden part of himself, a part buried so deep he hadn't thought it existed. Clearly it did, because he felt it all now: anger and guilt. Regret and fear. *Hurt.*

'All is not lost, Khalil,' Assad said quietly, dropping the honorific for once. 'Aziz is still not popular. Secretly marrying a servant will make him even less so.'

'Does that even matter?' Khalil bit out. 'He's fulfilled the terms of the will. He is Sheikh.'

'But very few people want him to be.'

'So you're suggesting a civil war,' Khalil stated flatly. 'I didn't think Aziz would go that far.' And he wasn't sure he would either, no matter what he'd thought before. Felt before.

Risking so much for his own crown, endangering his people, was not an option he wanted to consider now.

Things were changing. *They'd already changed.*

He wasn't the cold, ruthless man he'd once been, yet if he wasn't Sheikh...

What was he?

'A civil war is not the only option,' Assad said quietly. 'You could approach Aziz, demand a referendum.'

Khalil let out a mirthless laugh. 'He has everything he wants. Why would he agree?'

'There is something to be said for a fair fight, Your Highness,' Assad answered. 'Aziz might want to put the rumours and unrest behind him. If he wins the vote, his throne is secure.'

And Khalil would have no chance at all. He would have to accept defeat finally, totally—another option he didn't like to consider.

'There are a lot of people in Siyad,' he said with an attempt at wryness, and Assad smiled.

'There are a lot of people in the desert.'

'Aziz might not even agree to see me. We haven't seen each other since we were children.'

'You can try.'

'Yes.' He nodded slowly, accepting.

'You still have the stronger position,' Assad stated steadily. 'You always have. The people are loyal to you, not to Aziz.'

'I know that.' He felt his throat go tight. Did he really deserve such loyalty? And did he dare trust it? He knew how quickly someone could turn on you. Only the day before his father had thrown him out of the palace, he'd sat in on one of Khalil's lessons, had chucked him under the chin when Khalil had said his times tables.

Stupid, childish memories, yet still they hurt. They burned.

'So you will speak to Aziz?'

Khalil ran his fingers through his hair, his eyes gritty with fatigue. A thousand thoughts whirled through his mind, and one found purchase: one way forward, one way to solidify his position and strengthen his claim to the throne.

Now more than ever, he needed to marry Elena.

Aziz's bride. The woman the country had already accepted as the Sheikh's wife-to-be. The woman at least one tribe already thought was his wife.

He'd reacted so forcefully against it because he didn't want to risk his emotions or his heart. So, he wouldn't. Just like her, he couldn't afford to look for love. He'd keep a tight rein on his emotions and have the kind of marriage both he and Elena wanted: one of mutual benefit…and satisfaction.

Just the thought of being with Elena again sent desire arrowing through him.

'The servant is not even Kadaran,' Assad said quietly, and Khalil wondered if his friend and right- hand man had guessed the progression of his thoughts.

'Neither is Elena,' Khalil answered, and Assad smiled faintly. Khalil now knew he had been thinking along the same lines.

'She is a queen, an accepted choice. Marrying her would work in your favour.'

'I know.' Khalil took a deep breath, let it out slowly. 'I know.'

'Then…?'

'I'll go find her.' And by this time tomorrow, perhaps, he would be married.

The camp was quiet and dark all around him as Khalil walked towards Elena's tent. A strange mix of emotions churned within him: resolve, resignation and a little spark of excitement that he tried to suppress.

Yes, he would enjoy Elena's body again. But this would be a marriage of convenience. No more play-acting at love. No more pretending. No more *feeling*.

The guards stepped aside as he came to the tent and drew the curtain back—and stopped short when he saw Elena curled up on her bed, her face pressed into her pillow, sobbing as if her heart would break.

Or had already been broken…by him.

'Elena…Elena!'

Elena felt hard hands on her shoulders drawing her up from her damp pillow and then cradling her against an even harder chest.

Khalil. For a second she let herself enjoy the feel of him. Then she remembered that she'd been bawling her eyes out and twisted out of his embrace.

'You should have knocked,' she snapped, dashing the tears from her cheeks. She probably looked frightful, her face blotchy, her eyes red and swollen…

She sniffed. *And* her nose was running. Perfect.

'Knock?' Khalil repeated, one eyebrow raised in eloquent scepticism. 'On the flap of a tent?'

'You know what I mean,' she retorted. 'You should have made your presence known.'

Khalil regarded her quietly for a moment. 'You're right,' he finally said. 'I should have. I'm sorry.'

'Well.' She sniffed again, trying desperately for dignity. 'Thank you.'

'Why were you crying, Elena?'

She shook her head as if she could deny the overwhelming evidence of her tears. 'It's been a couple of very long days,' she muttered. 'I was… I'm just tired.'

'You weren't crying as if you were just tired.'

'Why do you care?' she demanded. Perhaps going on the offensive was best.

Khalil opened his mouth, then shut it again. 'I don't *care*,' he answered. 'But I want to know.'

'I've got a lot going on in my life that has nothing to do with you, Khalil. Maybe I'm crying about *that*.' She wasn't about to admit that she had been crying about him along with everything else that had gone wrong in her life.

'I wasn't assuming you were crying about me,' he stated quietly. His voice was calm but he sounded as if he was trying not to grit his teeth.

'Weren't you?' Elena retorted. 'Ever since spending the night together you've been completely paranoid that I'm obsessing over you, and I can assure you, I'm not.'

'What a relief.'

'Isn't it?'

They glared at each other. Elena folded her arms and tried to stare him down; Khalil's eyes sparked annoyance and his mouth was compressed.

'Why did you come into my tent, anyway?' she finally asked, their gazes still clashing. 'Have you learned something? Some news?'

'Yes, I have.'

Her stomach rolled and she felt her nails bite into her

palms. 'What have you heard? Has Markos called for a meeting?'

'I haven't heard any news from Thallia, Elena. I think they still believe you are safely with Aziz.' Khalil's mouth was still a hard line but his expression seemed softer somehow, his eyes almost sad. 'It's Aziz,' he said after a pause. 'He's married someone else, just like you said he would.'

'He has?' Her eyes widened as she considered what this meant for Khalil. 'He did it within the six weeks?'

'Yes.'

'Then he fulfilled…?'

'The terms of my father's will.' Khalil nodded. 'Yes, he did. But you…? You're not sad?'

She stared at him in disbelief. 'About Aziz? I gave up on him a while ago, Khalil.'

'Yes, but…still…he chose someone else. Rather quickly.'

'So did I.' She gave him a look filled with dark humour. 'At least Aziz received a positive answer to his proposal.'

'Yes…' He shook his head, almost as if to clear it. 'About that proposal…'

'Trust me, you don't need to remind me how much you don't want to marry me, Khalil. I got that the first time.'

'I'm sorry if I seemed…negative.'

She rolled her eyes. 'That's an understatement.' Better to joke than to cry. In any case, she wasn't sure she had any tears left, just a heavy sense of weariness, a resignation that nothing was going to be easy. That she'd probably lose her crown.

'You surprised me,' he said. 'I wasn't expecting… I've never expected…'

'I know.' She shook her head, exasperated, exhausted and definitely not needing to hash through all this again. 'Why are we even talking about this, Khalil?'

'Because,' he answered evenly, 'I've changed my mind.'

She blinked and then blinked again, the meaning of his words penetrating slowly. 'You've what?'

'I've changed my mind,' he repeated clearly. 'I want to marry you.'

Elena opened her mouth, then closed it again. 'Well,' she finally managed. 'That was a charming proposal.'

'Don't be absurd, Elena. This is about convenience, for both of us.'

'You didn't seem to think so an hour ago.'

'Aziz's marriage has made me realise I need to strengthen my position.'

'But if he's married,' Elena said slowly, 'he's fulfilled the terms of the will. How can you fight that?'

'I can't. I don't want to start a war. The only thing I can do is confront him openly—demand he call the referendum. Perhaps I should have done that before, but it seemed too easy for Aziz to refuse. Perhaps it still is.'

'And marrying me will strengthen your position when it comes to a vote.'

Khalil gazed at her evenly. 'Yes.'

'That's quite a sacrifice for you to make,' she said a bit sharply. 'Just to look good for a vote.'

'I am the rightful Sheikh, Elena,' Khalil said, his voice rising with the force of his conviction. 'That is who I *am*, who I always will be. I've lived my entire life waiting for the day I took the throne. Every choice I've made, every single thing I've done, has been to that end. Not for revenge, but for justice. Because it is right—' He broke off, forced a smile. 'In any case, marrying you is not a sacrifice.'

'No?'

'We are friends, are we not? And we have enjoyed each other's bodies. Neither of us wants anything more.' He smiled, reached out to touch her face. 'It's a match made in heaven.'

'That's an about-face if I've ever seen one,' she huffed.

'I admit, your proposal shocked me. I reacted emotionally rather than sensibly.'

'I didn't think you had emotions.'

'You know I do, Elena.' His gaze seemed to burn into hers. 'I will be honest. This—' he gestured between them '—scares me.'

Elena felt as if a giant fist had taken hold of her heart. 'It scares me too, Khalil.'

'So that is why we will agree to this convenient marriage,' he answered with a small smile. 'Because neither of us wants to be hurt again.'

'Right,' Elena agreed, but to her own ears her voice sounded hollow. They didn't want to be hurt again—but she wondered if she or Khalil would be able to keep themselves from it.

CHAPTER ELEVEN

ELENA GAZED OUT of the window of the royal jet at the perfect azure sky and marvelled at how quickly things had changed. Just forty-eight hours earlier she'd been sobbing into her pillow, stuck in the middle of the desert with no possibilities and no hope.

Now she was flying back to Thallia with Khalil by her side, planning a wedding in just a few days' time, and everything was possible.

Well, almost everything. She snuck a sideways glance at Khalil who sat opposite her, his face looking as if it had been chiselled from marble. A deep frown had settled between his brows and his mouth was its usual hard line. He'd barely spoken to her since he'd reconsidered her marriage proposal, a proposal which Elena had wondered more than once whether she should have accepted.

Yet in the moment before she'd agreed, when he'd been waiting for her answer, she'd seen a look of uncertainty on his face, almost as if he were bracing himself for a blow. As if he expected her to reject him.

That moment of vulnerability had been gone in an instant, but it still lingered in Elena's mind. In her heart. Because it made Khalil a man with softness and secrets, a man she was starting to understand and know better and better.

Which, Elena acknowledged, violated the terms of this very convenient marriage. It was what she had first suggested, after all. If some contrary, feminine part of her wanted something different, something more...well, too bad.

She had other, more important things to think about. Like the fact that she was going to face her Council in just a few hours, and with a different fiancé in tow. She glanced again at Khalil, grateful that he'd agreed to accompany her to Thallia and marry in a private ceremony in the palace. It had made sense, rather than something furtive and hurried in the desert; both of them wanted this marriage to be accepted by the public as quickly as possible.

After she'd presented him to her Council, they'd return to Siyad and Khalil would demand Aziz call the referendum. Khalil had told her Aziz had retreated with his bride to a remote royal palace for his honeymoon. The announcement from the palace had simply said the Sheikh had wed, not the name of his bride. Siyad buzzed with speculation, but no one knew what was really going on. Khalil had said Aziz was just buying time. Things would come to a head when they returned from Thallia and Elena hoped that both of their countries—and thrones—would be secure.

Even then she didn't know what life with Khalil would look like, or even where or how they would live. She and Aziz had discussed all these details, outlined everything in a twenty-page document that had been drawn up by lawyers from both of their countries.

But everything with Khalil was unknown. Looking at his grim expression, she wasn't sure she wanted to discuss it now.

Instead she tried to plan what she would say to her Council. To Markos. No doubt he'd be contemptuous of her sudden change of groom. Perhaps he would claim she was being deceived by Khalil, as she had been by Paulo.

She thought of all the things Markos could say, all the contempt he could pour on her, and in Khalil's presence, and inwardly she cringed.

'What's wrong?' Khalil asked, turning to fix her with a narrowed gaze, and Elena realised her reaction had been visible too.

'Nothing…' she began, only to acknowledge she would have to tell Khalil about her mistakes. Better to hear it from her than Markos.

And actually, she realised, she *wanted* to tell him. She wanted to be honest, to share her burden with someone. To trust him with the truth.

'Elena?' Khalil prompted, and she took a deep breath.

'Khalil…I need to tell you some things.'

His gaze swept over her. 'All right.'

Elena took another deep breath. She wanted to tell Khalil, but it was still hard. 'I was young when I became queen,' she began. 'As you know. My parents had just died and I suppose I was feeling…vulnerable. Lonely.'

'Of course you were, Elena.' His face softened in sympathy. 'You'd had an isolated childhood and then you lost the two people who were closest to you.'

'Even if they weren't all that close.'

'Still, they were your parents. You loved them, and they loved you.'

'Yes.' She nodded, feeling a sudden, surprising peace about what Khalil had so simply and surely stated. Her parents had loved her. No matter how little they might have shown it during their lives, they'd loved her in their own way.

'So what happened when you became queen?' he asked after a moment, his voice gentle, and Elena gave him a rather shaky smile.

'My mother's brother, Paulo, came to stay with me after the funeral. I hadn't known him very well—he spent most of his time in Paris or Monte Carlo. I don't think my father liked him all that much. He'd stayed away, in any case.'

'And after the funeral?'

'He was very kind to me.' She sighed, a weary acceptance and regret coursing through her. 'He was funny and charming and in some ways he felt like the father I'd never had. The one I'd always wanted. Approachable. Genuine. Or so I thought.'

'He wasn't, I presume.' Khalil's frown deepened. 'This is the man who betrayed you.'

'Yes, he did, yet I trusted him. I listened to him, and I came to him for advice. The Council didn't want me to rule—Andreas Markos had tried to appoint himself as Regent.'

'But you're of age.'

'He made the case that I didn't have enough political experience. And he was right, you know. I didn't. I'd gone to a few royal functions, a few balls and events and things. But I didn't have the first clue about laws or policies. About anything real or important.'

'You learned, though. I've read some of the bills you helped draft online, Elena. You're not a pretty princess sitting on her throne, you're an active head of government.'

'Not at first.'

'The Council should have given you time to adjust to your new role.'

'Well, they didn't, not really.'

Khalil shook his head. 'So what happened with Paulo?'

'He advised me on some real-estate deals: government subsidies for tourist developments on our coastal region. I thought he was helping me, but he was just lining his own pockets.'

'How could you have known?'

'It wasn't just that,' she hastened to explain, practically tripping over herself to tell him the whole sordid truth. She needed him to know, craved for him to accept the whole of her and what she'd done. 'Every piece of advice he gave me was to benefit himself. And there were worse things. He forged my signature on cheques. He even stole some of my mother's jewels, which weren't hers to begin with. They were part of the crown jewels and they belonged to the government.'

She closed her eyes, filled with remorse and shame. 'I was completely clueless, pathetically grateful for all his support. Markos uncovered it, and had him sent to prison. Kept the scandal from breaking in the press, thankfully— not for my sake, but for Thallia's.'

'That must have been very hard.'

'Yes.' Her throat was so tight it hurt to speak, but she kept going. 'You know what's really sad? Sometimes I still miss him. He completely betrayed me in every way possible, and I actually miss him.' She shook her head, suddenly near tears, and Khalil reached over and covered her hand with his own.

'He seemed kind to you, and during a time when you craved that kindness. Of course you miss that.'

'Do you miss your father?' she blurted, and Khalil stilled, his hand tensing over hers.

'I've hated my father for so long,' he said slowly. 'And I can't ever forget what he did.' His face contorted for a second, and she knew how difficult this was for him to admit. 'But I do miss his kindness to me. His—his love.'

'Of course you do,' she murmured and Khalil gave her a wry and rather shaky smile.

'I never realised that before. I was too busy being angry.'

'Are you still angry?'

'I don't know what I am,' he said, sounding both surprised and confused, and then he shook his head. 'We weren't talking about me, though. We were talking about you. You shouldn't blame yourself, Elena, for trusting a man who did his best to endear himself to you.'

'I should have known better.'

Khalil shook his head, his hand tightening on hers. 'You were young and vulnerable. It wasn't your fault.'

'The Council thinks it was. Or, at the very least, it completely undermined any confidence they might have had in me. Markos has been working steadily to discredit me ever since.'

Khalil frowned. 'How?'

'Rumours, whispers. Gossip that I'm flighty, forgetful. So far I've managed to keep him from destabilising me completely. I hope—I hope my record speaks for itself.' She turned to him, needing him to believe her just as he had once needed her to believe him. 'I've worked hard since the whole Paulo debacle, Khalil. I've poured my life into my country, just as my father wanted me to. Everything I've done has been for Thallia.'

'I know it has,' Khalil said quietly. He squeezed her hand. 'Your devotion to your country is something I've never questioned.' He gave her a small smile. 'After all, you were willing to marry for it.'

'As were you.'

'Hopefully it was a wise decision on both our parts.' He removed his hand from hers and sat back, his brow furrowed.

Elena suspected he regretted the intimacy of their conversation. She knew that wasn't part of their marriage deal. And yet, watching him covertly, remembering how her body yearned and her heart ached for him, Elena wondered how she could have fooled herself into thinking she'd ever be satisfied with a marriage of convenience.

With Aziz it had been different. He'd been a stranger, and she'd given little thought to their marriage beyond the hard practicalities. Now she wondered how she could have been so blind. So naïve. How could she have coped with such a cold approach to marriage, to motherhood? *How would she now?*

She stared out of the window, realisations trickling despondently through her. She didn't want a loveless arrangement any more. She wanted more from her marriage. More from Khalil.

She glanced back at Khalil; he looked distant and pre-occupied. The things she wanted now seemed more unlikely than ever.

Khalil stared out of the window as the jet descended towards the runway, the waters of the Aegean Sea sparkling jewel-bright in the distance. He could see the domes and towers of Thallia's ancient capital, the sky a bright blue above, the sun bathing everything in gold.

He turned to look at Elena and saw how pale she'd gone, her hands clenched together in her lap so tightly her knuckles shone bony and white. He felt a shaft of sympathy for her, deep and true, in that moment. She'd endured so much, yet had stayed so strong, even if she didn't think she was. Even if she didn't trust herself.

He trusted her. He believed in her, believed in her strength, her courage, her goodness. The knowledge made something in him break open, seek light. He leaned forward and reached for her hand. She turned to him, clearly startled, her eyes wide with apprehension.

'You're stronger than they are, Elena,' he said quietly. 'And smarter. They may think you need me, but you don't. You are a legitimate and admirable ruler all on your own.'

Her cheeks went pink and her eyes turned shiny. For a moment Khalil thought she might cry. Then her lips curved in a wobbly smile and she said, 'Thank you, Khalil. But you're wrong—I do need you. I needed you to tell me that.'

They left the plane, blinking in the bright sunlight as they took the stairs down to the waiting motorcade. The paparazzi, thankfully, weren't present; Elena had told him there would be a press briefing from the palace after they met with her Council.

He hadn't liked leaving Kadar, but he understood the necessity of it. A marriage made deep in the desert was essentially no marriage at all. They both needed the positive publicity, the statement their marriage would make not just to Elena's Council but to Aziz.

I took your bride. I'll take your throne. Because both are mine by right.

Khalil felt the old injustice burn, but not as brightly or hotly as it had before. In that moment, looking at her pale face, he was more concerned for Elena than anything that was happening in Kadar. The realisation surprised him, yet he didn't fight it, didn't push the feelings away. He reached for Elena's hand once more and she clung to him, her fingers slender and icy in his.

'Welcome back to Thallia, Your Highness.'

Khalil watched Elena greet the royal staff who had lined up by the fleet of cars. She nodded and spoke to each one by name, smiling graciously, her head held high.

She looked pale but composed, elegant and every inch the queen despite the fear he knew she had to be feeling. Admiration and something deeper swelled inside him. Queen Elena of Thallia was magnificent.

Two hours later they were at the palace, waiting outside the Council Room. Elena had changed into a modest dress in blue silk, feminine yet businesslike, her heavy, dark hair pulled back in a low coil. Khalil wore an elegantly tailored business suit and, as they waited to be admitted to the Council Room, he wondered what this Markos was playing at. Was he keeping Elena waiting on purpose, to unnerve her? A petty show of power? Based on what Elena had already told him, it seemed likely.

He turned to Elena. 'You should go in there.'

'I'm meant to wait until I'm summoned.'

'You are Queen, Elena. You do the summoning.'

'It's not like that, Khalil.'

'It should be. You're the one who can change things, Elena. Remember that. *Believe* it.'

She stared at him uncertainly for a moment and he imagined how hard it must have been for her, all of nineteen years old, devastated by grief and so utterly alone, trying to assert herself against the sanctimonious prigs of her Council. The fact that she was still here, still strong, both amazed and humbled him.

'You can do it,' he said softly. 'You can do anything you set your mind to, Elena. I know that. I've seen it.'

She gave him a small, tremulous smile. 'Except maybe make a fire in the middle of the desert.'

He felt himself grin back at her. 'There were a few flames going there. If that snake hadn't come along...'

'If you hadn't come along,' she shot back, her smile widening, and then she drew herself up and turned towards the double gold-panelled doors.

He watched as she threw open the doors, grinned at the sight of twelve slack-jawed, middle-aged men rising hastily to their feet as Elena walked into the room.

'Good afternoon, gentlemen,' she greeted them regally, and Khalil had to keep from letting out a cheer.

Elena could feel her heart thudding so hard it hurt and she could hear the roar of her blood in her ears. She kept her head high, her smile polite and fixed, as she gazed at each member of the Council in turn, saving Markos for last. Her nemesis's eyes were narrowed, the corners of his mouth turned down, and she felt a flash of relief. If he'd made any headway with the rest of the Council, he'd have been looking at her in triumph, not irritation. She was safe...so far.

'Queen Elena. We have been wondering where you had gone.' Marko's gaze flicked to Khalil. 'A honeymoon in the desert?' he suggested with only the faintest hint of a sneer, but as always it was enough. He made it sound as if she'd run off with her bodyguard, heedless of her country or its demands.

'There has been no honeymoon yet,' Elena answered crisply. 'But things, as you have surmised, have changed. I wisely ended my engagement to Aziz al Bakir when I realised he was not the legitimate claimant to the throne of Kadar. Marriage to an impostor would hardly benefit Thallia, would it…Andreas?'

Markos's eyes flashed annoyance or perhaps even anger. 'And who is this, then?' he asked, his gaze flicking back to Khalil.

'This is Khalil al Bakir, sheikh of a northern desert tribe and Aziz's older brother. He is the rightful heir to the throne of Kadar.' Elena felt the sudden surprise tense Khalil's body, felt it in herself. She'd spoken with a certainty she felt right through her bones.

'I have chosen to marry Khalil instead, in an arrangement similar to the one I had with Aziz.' She looked at each councillor in turn, felt herself practically grow taller. Khalil had been right. She was strong and smart enough, yet she was still achingly glad he was by her side. 'I trust that this will be agreeable to all of you, as it was before?'

'You change husbands at the drop of a hat,' Markos said, his lip curling in contempt. 'And we are meant to take you at your word?'

For a second Elena felt herself falter, everything in her an apology for past sins, but in her moment of damning silence Khalil spoke. 'Yes,' he stated coolly. 'As she is your queen and sovereign, you will most certainly take her at her word. Queen Elena has demonstrated her loyalty to her country again and again. It will not be called into question simply because once long ago she gave her trust and her loyalty to a man who should have, by all measures, been worthy of it.' Elena watched in amazement as Khalil nailed each councillor with a hard, challenging stare. 'We will not speak of this again. Ever.'

She barely heard the answering buzz of murmured assurances and apologies; her mind was spinning from what Khalil had said, how he'd stood up for her, supported her. When had someone last done that?

She'd kept herself apart, refused to trust anyone, because it had felt stronger. Certainly less risky. But in that moment she knew she was actually stronger with Khalil, and the knowledge both thrilled and humbled her.

She turned to her Council with a cool, purposeful smile. 'Now, shall we discuss the meeting with the press?'

CHAPTER TWELVE

ELENA CLOSED THE door quietly behind her and leaned against it, her eyes closed, exhaustion making every muscle and sinew ache. It had been a long, stressful, overwhelming and yet ultimately successful day.

She hadn't had a chance to tell Khalil how grateful she was for his support, from the showdown with the Council to his effortless grace and charm before the press. It had been a tense diplomatic moment, supporting Khalil's claim to Kadar's throne publicly, and one her Council had initially balked at. But Khalil had stood by her and it was her turn to stand by him.

Side by side. That was the kind of marriage she wanted. And today it had felt as if Khalil wanted it too.

Maybe all he needed was time to get used to the idea, to learn to love again…

Because she loved him. It had been utter foolishness to pretend she didn't, or wouldn't. She'd been fooling herself as well as Khalil, but now she wanted to be honest. Wanted to admit her feelings for him, her love, respect and desire.

Yes, desire. She'd felt it all day like an in-coming tide, lapping at her senses, washing over her body. Every aspect of him appealed to her, from his hard-headed pragmatism to his sudden sensitivity, to that sensual blaze of heat in his eyes…

They hadn't spoken privately since the plane, since she'd told him about Paulo—and she'd seen no judgement or condemnation in his eyes, just understanding and a surprising compassion, which just added to her desire. He was, she'd realised, not for the first time but with growing certainty, a *good* man.

After the press conference he'd gone to deal with matters relating to Kadar, and she had met with her personal assistant to review the schedule for the next few days. A team of lawyers had hammered out an agreement concerning the marriage terms that they'd both signed, and then they'd eaten dinner with a handful of dignitaries before parting ways, Khalil to a guest suite in another wing and she to her own suite of rooms.

Already she missed him. She needed to talk to him, she realised; they'd set the wedding for tomorrow and yet had barely discussed the details beyond a clinical meeting with the legal team. In any case, she didn't want to talk business; she just wanted to be with him.

Swiftly she turned around and opened the door, slipped from her room and down several corridors to where she knew Khalil was staying.

She stood in front of his door, her palms slightly damp and her heart beginning to race. She knocked.

'Enter.'

Elena stepped inside and the whole world seemed to fall away as her gaze focused on Khalil. He'd undone the studs of his tuxedo shirt, its tails untucked from his trousers so she could see a bronzed expanse of taut belly, and her breath instinctively hitched.

Khalil's gaze darkened, although with what emotion she couldn't tell. 'I thought you were one of the staff.'

'No.'

A tiny smile twitched at the corner of his mouth. 'I realise.'

Hope ballooned inside her, impossible to control. One smile and she was lost. 'I thought we should talk.'

'About?'

'We're getting married tomorrow, Khalil,' she reminded him with a smile, and his smile deepened.

'I know that, Elena.' He turned to face her fully, his arms folded across that magnificently broad chest. 'Are you having second thoughts? Cold feet?'

Surprise at his question, and the shadow of vulnerability that crossed his face, made her shake her head decisively. 'No.' She took a breath and forced her gaze away from his pectorals. 'Are you?'

'No.'

'Even though you didn't want to marry?'

She shouldn't have pressed, Elena realised. Any levity they'd been flirting with disappeared in an instant. 'You know my feelings on the subject.'

'A necessary evil?'

He inclined his head. 'That might be a bit harsh.'

Elena rolled her eyes, inviting him into the joke, wanting to reclaim the lightness. 'Well, that's a relief.'

He smiled again and Elena felt a giddy rush of joy. She really did love his smile. She loved...

But she wouldn't tell him that now. She knew he wasn't ready to hear it, and she wasn't sure she was ready to say it.

'Why are you here, Elena?' Khalil asked quietly.

'I told you, to talk.'

He took a step towards her, his muscles rippling under his open shirt, his eyes glinting gold with amusement—and knowledge. 'Are you sure about that?'

Suddenly her mouth was dry. Her heart beat harder. 'No,' she whispered.

He took another step towards her and then another, so if she lifted her hand she could touch him. He smiled down at her. 'I didn't think so.'

Of course he didn't think so. Her need for him was obvious, overwhelming and undeniable. And the very force of it made her bold. 'I want you, Khalil.'

Appreciation flared in his eyes. 'I want you too.'

Want. So basic, so huge, yet Elena felt even more than just that. She felt gratitude and admiration, respect and joy, all because of what he'd done, who he was. How he'd helped and strengthened her. She'd never expected to feel that way about someone, to have that person fulfil a need and hope in her she hadn't even known she had.

The need to tell him all that she felt was an ache in her chest, a pressure building inside her, so she opened her mouth to speak, to say even just a fraction of what was in her heart.

But Khalil didn't let her.

He curled his hands around her shoulders and drew her to him, stealing her words away with a kiss. It was better this way, Elena had to acknowledge as she lost herself in the heady sensations. Khalil didn't want her words, her declarations of emotion. He just wanted this.

And so did she.

He drew her to the bed and down upon the silken sheets, stripping the evening gown from her body with one gentle tug of the zip. Neither of them spoke, and the silence felt hushed, reverent. This time tomorrow they would lie in a bed like this one as husband and wife.

But Elena knew she already felt like Khalil's wife in her mind, in her heart. She cared too much for him, she knew, but in this moment, when his hands were touching her with such tenderness and his mouth was on hers, she didn't want to think about *too much*. She didn't want to police herself, or limit her joy. She just wanted to experience all Khalil was offering her…however little that turned out to be.

And, in that moment, it felt like enough.

Afterwards they lay entwined among the sheets, her palm resting over his heart so she could feel its steady thud against her hand. Khalil stroked her arm from shoulder to wrist, almost absently, the touch unthinking and yet incredibly gentle. She felt almost perfectly happy.

If only, she thought, they could stay like this for ever.

It was a foolish wish, nothing more than a dream, yet she was so tired of the scheming and trying, the politics and the uncertainty. She just wanted this. Him. *For ever.*

'When will you speak with Aziz?' she asked softly, because no matter what she wanted reality had to be faced.

'As soon as we return to Kadar I will seek out a meeting. He will hear of our marriage, of course, and I will have to address that.'

'Do you think he'll be angry?'

She felt Khalil tense, and then he shrugged. 'I have no idea. You know him better than I do.'

'I do?' She raised her head, propping herself on one elbow to study his face. 'Did you not know him as a child?'

'I left the palace when I was seven. I only met him once, from memory, when my father wished for his sons to see each other.'

He spoke evenly, but she could still feel the tension in his body, under her hand. She gazed at him, realising afresh how much she didn't know...and how much she wanted to.

'It must have been very hard,' she said softly. 'To have to leave everything you knew.'

'It was strange,' Khalil acknowledged. His expression had become shuttered, his eyes giving nothing away.

She eased away from him so she could look up into his face. 'I know you don't like to talk about it, Khalil, but what happened with your father must have been terrible.' Her gaze fell on the scars that crisscrossed his wrists. 'Why do you have rope burns on your wrists?' she asked softly.

She thought he wouldn't answer. He didn't speak for a long time, and she wondered at the story those scars told, a story she had no idea about but knew she wanted and perhaps even needed to hear.

'I was tied up,' he said finally, his voice flat, emotionless. 'For days. I struggled, and these scars are the result.'

She stared at him in helpless horror. 'Tied up? When—?'

'When I was seven. When my father banished me.'

'But I thought you went to America with your aunt.'

'She found me when I was ten. For three years I lived with a Bedouin tribe in a far corner of Kadar. The sheikh liked to punish me. He'd tie me up like a dog, or beat me in front of everyone. I tried to escape, and I always failed. So, believe me, I understood how you felt as a prisoner, Elena. More than you could possibly know.' He let out a shuddering breath and unthinkingly, just needing to touch him, she wrapped her arms around him, held on tight.

'I'm sorry.'

'It was a long time ago.'

'But something like that stays with you for ever, Khalil!' She remembered now how he'd told her it mattered how she was treated. 'But this man, this sheikh—why did he treat you so terribly?'

Khalil gave a little shrug. 'Because he was a petty, evil man and he could? But, no, the real reason I suppose is because my mother was his cousin and she brought shame to his family with her alleged adultery. In any case, Abdul-Hafiz already had a grudge against her family for leaving the tribe and seeking their fortunes in Siyad.' His arms tightened around her. 'That's why my father banished me to that tribe—he returned me to my mother's people, knowing they would revile me. And so they did, at least at first. The irony, perhaps, is that I rule them now as their sheikh.'

He was trying to speak lightly but she still heard the throb of emotion underneath. Elena couldn't even imagine all he wasn't saying: the abuse, the torture and utter unkindness. To tie up a seven-year-old boy for *days*? To beat him so his back was covered with scars? Fury warred with deep sorrow, and she pressed her cheek against his back, her body snug against his.

'I'm so glad you escaped.'

'So am I.'

Yet could anyone really escape such a terrible past? Elena knew Khalil bore as many scars on his heart as he did on his wrists and back. No wonder he didn't trust anyone. No wonder he had no use or understanding of loving relationships.

Could she be the one to change him? Save him?

She shied away from such questions, knowing how dangerous they were, yet already the answers were rushing through her.

Yes. Yes, she could. She wanted to try, she needed to try, because she loved him and couldn't imagine a life without him. Without him loving her.

And she began in that moment, rolling onto her stomach and pressing her lips to his wrist, kissing the places where he'd been hurt the most. Underneath her, she felt Khalil shudder.

'Elena…'

She kissed her way across his body, touching every scar, taking her time with her tongue and her lips, savouring him, showing her love for him with her body because she couldn't with her words. Not yet.

And Khalil accepted her touch, his hands coming up to clutch her shoulders as she moved over him and then gently, wonderfully, sank onto him, taking him into her body, filling them both up to the brim with wonder and joy and pleasure.

His eyes closed and his breath came out in a shudder as she began to move, pouring out everything in her heart in that ultimate act of love—and praying Khalil understood what she was saying with her body.

Sleep was a long time coming that night. Khalil stared up at the canopied bed, his arms around Elena as her breathing evened out, and he wondered why on earth he'd told her so much, had said things he hadn't admitted to anyone, not even Dimah or Assad. He hated to think of anyone knowing the truth of his utter humiliation as a child, yet he'd willingly told Elena. In that moment he'd wanted to, had wanted someone to understand and accept him totally.

And her response had nearly undone him. The sweet selflessness of her touch, the giving of her body... He still wasn't sure he knew what love was, but he imagined it might feel like that. And, if it did, he wanted more. He wanted to love someone and know he was loved back.

Foolish, foolish, foolish. Insanity. This was a marriage of cold convenience, not love or trust or intimacy. He'd told Elena he wanted none of that, and he'd meant it.

How had he changed?

Yet he knew he had. He'd been changing since the moment he'd met her, since he'd seen a reflection of himself in her. She'd begun changing him even then, softening him, opening up his emotions, unlocking his heart.

How could he go back to the cold, barren life he'd once known?

How could he not?

He'd learned to trust her with so many things—with his feelings. With the truth. Could he trust her with his heart?

Their wedding took place in the palace chapel, with only the Council members and their wives, as well as a few ambassadors and diplomats, in attendance.

Elena wore a cream silk sheath dress and a matching fascinator, no veil or bouquet, or really anything bridal at all. She'd picked the outfit with the help of her stylist when she'd arrived in Thallia, thinking only of what image she wanted to present to her public. She'd wanted to seem like a woman in control of her country and her destiny, perfectly prepared to begin this businesslike marriage.

She hadn't wanted to look like a woman in love, yet she knew now that was what she was. And as she turned to Khalil to say her vows she wished, absurdly, perhaps, for a meringue of a dress and a great, big bouquet, a lovely lace veil and a father to give her away.

Never mind, she told herself. *It's the marriage that matters, not the wedding.* Yet what kind of marriage would she have with Khalil?

Last night had been so tender, so wonderful and intimate in every way, physically and emotionally. Yet this morning he seemed his usual, inscrutable self, stony-faced and silent, dressed in traditional Kadaran formal wear, a richly embroidered *thobe* and loose trousers. He looked magnificent—and a little frightening, because Elena had no idea what he was thinking or feeling.

The ceremony passed in a blur. Vows were spoken, words read, then Khalil drew her to him and pressed his mouth against hers in a cool kiss.

She still had no idea what was going on behind those veiled eyes.

Elena circulated through the guests at a small reception after the ceremony, her gaze tracking Khalil's movements around the room, even as she chatted with councillors who oozed satisfaction now that she was wed and taken care of.

She felt as if everything had changed for her—but had it for him? Should she even hope it had? It might be better—wiser, safer—not to let things change for herself. Not to open herself up to all of the pain and possibility that loving someone meant.

It was too late for that, she knew. She couldn't stop what she felt for Khalil, just as she couldn't keep the waves from crashing into the sea or the moon from rising that night. Her love for him simply *was.*

After the reception they retired to a suite of rooms in its own private wing, as much of a bridal chamber as the palace had.

Elena took in the champagne chilling by the canopied bed, the fire crackling in the fireplace, the frothy nightgown some accommodating member of staff had laid out for her.

'It's all a bit much, isn't it?' she said with an attempt at wryness. She felt, bizarrely, as if they were pretending, as if they were going through the motions of marriage and love when last night she'd felt they'd known the real thing.

'It's thoughtful,' Khalil answered with a shrug. He hesitated, his gaze pinned to hers even though Elena had no idea what he felt or what he intended to say. 'You looked beautiful today. You still do.'

A thrill of surprised pleasure rippled through her. 'Thank you.'

'I couldn't take my eyes off you.'

'I couldn't take my eyes off you, either,' she admitted with a shy smile.

His answering smile was assured. 'I know.'

'Oh—you!' Elena gasped with a shocked laugh. 'You sound unbearably arrogant, you know.'

'But it's true.'

'It would be more gentlemanly for you not to remark on it.'

'Why?' he asked as he reached for her. 'When the feeling is mutual?'

She stared up at him, suddenly breathless. *Just how much was mutual?*

He feathered a few kisses along her jaw. 'And this is what I've been wanting to do all day long.'

'Why didn't you, then?' Elena managed as she tilted her head back to give him greater access.

Khalil pressed a kiss to the tender hollow of her throat. 'What do you think your stuffy councillors would have thought if I'd dragged you out of that ballroom and returned you with messed hair, swollen lips and a very big smile on your face?'

Elena let out a choked laugh, her mind blurring as Khalil's mouth moved lower. 'I think they would have been pleased. I'd have been put in my place as a dutiful wife.'

'I like the sound of those duties,' Khalil answered as he

tugged at the zip of her dress. 'I think you need more instruction on just how to carry them out.'

Her dress slithered down her body, leaving her in nothing but her bra and pants, her whole body on fire from the heat of Khalil's gaze. 'I think I do,' she agreed…then they didn't speak for quite a while after that.

Later they lay in bed just as they had last night, hands linked and limbs entwined. Sleepily, utterly sated, Elena thought how this did feel like for ever. Maybe they could be this happy…for ever.

'I need to go to Paris,' Khalil said. His fingers tightened briefly on hers as he stared up at the bed's canopy. 'To see my Aunt Dimah. She moved there a few years ago. She should hear of our marriage from me. And I'd like you to meet her.'

'Of course,' Elena said simply. She was glad to share in any part of Khalil's life that he wanted her to.

'And after that,' he continued, 'we will return to Kadar. I received a message from Aziz today, just before the wedding. He has agreed to meet with me.'

'That's good news, isn't it?'

'I hope it is. I hope I will be able to convince him to call the referendum.'

'And if he refuses?'

Khalil stared up at the ceiling. 'I don't know,' he said quietly. 'I don't—I don't want war. But I can't imagine giving up my claim to the throne, either. It's everything to me.' He turned to her then, a new, raw vulnerability shadowing his eyes. 'Not everything,' he amended. 'Not any more. But it's important, Elena.'

'I know it is.'

'Everything I've been, everything I've done, has been for Kadar. For my title.'

'I know,' she said softly. She leaned over and kissed him. 'I know how important this is, Khalil, and I believe in you just as you've believed in me. You'll succeed. You'll convince Aziz and win the vote.'

He smiled and squeezed her fingers. 'I pray so.'

'I know it.'

'I'd like you to be with me when the referendum is called,' Khalil said after a moment. 'It's important for the people to see you support me. But it shouldn't take long, and afterwards you can return to Thallia. Those were the terms of our agreement.'

Elena thought of the soulless piece of paper they'd both signed just yesterday, outlining the nature of their marriage: so cold, so clinical. She felt his fingers threaded through hers, his legs tangled with hers, and she mentally consigned that piece of paper and all of its legalese to the rubbish heap. 'I'll need to return to Thallia, of course,' she said. 'But do you want me to stay longer?' She twisted to face him, and was gratified to see a light blaze in Khalil's eyes.

'Yes,' he said simply, and she squeezed his hand, never feeling more certain of anything in her life. She loved this man and she would go anywhere with him.

'Then I'll stay,' she said simply, and Khalil closed the space between them and kissed her.

CHAPTER THIRTEEN

THE NEXT MORNING they boarded the royal jet to Paris. Since last night Elena had felt closer to Khalil than ever before, even though neither of them had put a name to what they felt. Perhaps it was too early to put such fragile feelings into words; in any case, Elena was simply glad to be sharing Khalil's life, and that he wanted her to.

'You must be very close to your aunt,' she said as the plane took off and they settled into their seats. A royal steward brought a tray of coffee and pastries into the main cabin.

Khalil poured milk into both of their coffees, his mouth twisting in something like a grimace. 'I am, but it is a complicated relationship.'

'How so?'

'When Dimah found me, I'd been in the desert for three years. I was...' He paused, his gaze on the bright blue sky visible from the plane's windows. 'Difficult. No, that is putting a polite spin on it—feral is a better description.'

Feral. Elena swallowed and blinked back sudden tears. Emotions, ones she'd suppressed and denied for so long, were always so close to the surface now; Khalil had made her feel, want and love again. 'I hate to think of what you endured, Khalil.'

'It was a long time ago,' he answered. 'But I admit, it affected me badly. I'd been treated like an animal for three years, so even after Dimah found me I acted like one. I didn't trust anyone. I barely spoke.' He shook his head, his features tightening. 'She was very patient. She took me to New York to live with her and her husband. She brought me to learning specialists and therapists, people who helped me adjust to this strange new life.'

'And you did adjust?'

Khalil grimaced. 'Some. But I haven't ever felt truly at home in America. No one understood me, or knew what I experienced. Not even really Dimah.'

'Did you tell her?'

'A little. I don't think she really wanted to know. She wanted me to forget Kadar completely, but returning to claim my birthright has always been what has motivated me. Dimah has never understood that.'

Surprise flashed through her. 'Why not?'

'The memories are too painful for her, I suppose. She grew up in Siyad, but she always longed to leave. When my mother died, she was heartbroken. She left to marry an American businessman and never wanted to return.'

'But she knows it is your right.'

'What she knows is that she provided a good life for me in America. She sent me to boarding school and university, helped me start my own consulting business before I joined the French Foreign Legion. She thought all those things would help me to forget Kadar, but I always saw them as stepping stones to returning. I don't think she has ever understood how much it has meant to me.'

'And yet the two of you are close,' Elena said quietly. 'Aren't you?'

'Yes, we are close. She saved me, quite literally.' The smile he gave her was bleak. 'I owe her a debt I can never repay, and I hope that one day she understands that I am attempting to redress it by claiming my birthright and becoming Sheikh.'

'Even though she doesn't want you to.'

'Yes.' He paused, his gaze moving once more to the

sky. 'Claiming my rightful inheritance will expunge any stain from my mother's memory. It's not just for my sake that I am pursuing this path. It's to right old wrongs, to repair the very fabric of my country that was torn when my father decided to pursue his own selfish whims instead of justice. Putting aside my mother with no real reason rent the country in two. I want to repair it.'

'And I want to help you, Khalil,' Elena said. She reached over and took his hand, and he squeezed her fingers in response. Encouraged by this show of affection, she took a deep breath and said some of what was in her heart. 'I know we agreed to live virtually separate lives in that document we signed, but I don't want to live that way any more.' She gazed into Khalil's clear, amber eyes, unable to tell what he thought about what she'd just said. 'You once asked me whether I wanted a loving, equal partner for a husband, someone who could support me. I said I didn't because I'd never even imagined someone like that existed.'

'Neither did I,' Khalil answered quietly and her hopes soared.

'Then you feel differently now too?'

'I don't know what I feel, Elena. I never expected or wanted any of this.' He sighed restlessly, but didn't let go of her hand. 'I feel like I've experienced something with you that I never thought I would. I want more of it. More of you. More of *us*.'

'I want that too,' she whispered.

'But this is all new to me. And frankly it's frightening.' He gave her a wry smile, but she still saw bleakness in his eyes. 'I haven't trusted anyone like this since I was seven years old with a child's simple heart. Since my father told me I wasn't his son.'

'I know, Khalil. And I want to be worthy of your trust and—and even of your love.' She held her breath, waiting for his reaction, wanting him to say it back: *I love you*. She hadn't said it quite as clearly as that, but still she thought he must know how she felt.

'I want to trust you,' Khalil answered after a long moment. He took a deep breath, squeezing her fingers once more. 'I want to love you.'

And in that moment it seemed so wonderfully simple, the way forward so very clear. They both wanted a loving relationship, a proper marriage. Why shouldn't they have it? Why shouldn't it be possible?

As they left the airport for Dimah's townhouse near the Ile de la Cité Khalil marvelled at the change in himself. He felt like some shell-less creature, pink, raw and exposed, everything out there for another person's examination. It was a strange and uncomfortable feeling, but it wasn't necessarily *bad*.

He'd been glad to tell Elena about his childhood, his aunt, his own fears and weaknesses. He'd never talked that way to another soul, yet he craved that kind of honesty with Elena.

He just didn't know what to do next. How it all would actually *work*. Take one step at a time, he supposed. For now he needed to think about Dimah.

He'd phoned her from Thallia, so she was waiting as their limo drew up to her townhouse and their security detail quickly got out to check the surrounding area.

Dimah came out to the front steps, her face wreathed in a tremulous smile, her wispy white hair blowing in the breeze. She looked so much older, Khalil thought with a pang, and he'd last seen her less than a year ago when he'd stopped in Paris on the way to Kadar.

'Dimah.' He put his arms around her, feeling her fragility. 'This is my wife, Queen Elena of Thallia.'

'Your Highness,' Dimah murmured and curtseyed. No matter how frail she looked or felt, she was still every inch the lady.

'I'm so pleased to meet you,' Elena said, and took Dimah's thin hand in both of her own.

Once inside, Dimah arranged for refreshments to be brought to the main salon, chattering with Elena about women's things while Khalil's mind roved over his arranged meeting with Aziz next week.

He'd been amazed that his half-brother had agreed to meet with him; it had given him hope. Perhaps Aziz really would see sense. Perhaps he would call the referendum.

And what about his wife?

Perhaps a quick and quiet annulment would get the nameless woman Aziz had married out of the way. Yet the fact that Aziz had been willing to marry so quickly made Khalil uneasy. It made him wonder if his half-brother wished to be Sheikh more than he'd thought he did.

'Khalil, you are not even paying attention,' Dimah chided. Her eyes were bright, her cheeks flushed. 'But I don't blame you. Anyone can tell you are in love!'

He felt Elena start next to him, saw her glance apprehensively at him. Was she worried for his sake or her own? He smiled and reached for her hand. It felt amazingly easy. 'You're right, Dimah,' he said. 'My mind is elsewhere.'

Elena beamed.

'I'm afraid I must excuse myself,' he said a few minutes later as he rose from his chair. 'I have business to attend to. But we will dine with you tonight, Dimah, if that is acceptable?'

She waved a hand in easy dismissal. 'Of course, of course. Go ahead. I want to get to know Elena properly.'

Suppressing a wry smile, Khalil gave his bride a look of sympathy before striding from the room.

'I can't tell you how pleased I am Khalil has found you,' Dimah said once she was alone with Elena. 'Anyone can tell how in love you are.'

Elena smiled, felt that tremulous joy buoy her soul.

'Do you think so?' she murmured, craving the confirmation of Khalil's feelings. 'I want to love you' was, she acknowledged, a little different from 'I love you'.

'I know it,' Dimah declared. 'I've waited so long for Khalil to find someone to love, and to love him back. I pray now he'll forget all this foolishness with Kadar.'

Elena tensed, unsure how to address such a volatile subject. 'The sheikhdom of Kadar is his legacy, Dimah,' she said gently. 'It's his birthright. He will not forget it.'

'He should,' Dimah said, her voice rising fretfully. 'He *should*. I keep telling him. There is nothing good for him there.' She bit her lip, her eyes filling with tears, and Elena frowned.

'Why do you want him to forget it?' she asked. 'Wouldn't you like to see him restored to his rightful place, and your sister's memory—'

'No.' Dimah cut her off swiftly. 'No. We mustn't talk about that.' She shook her head, seeming to come to herself. 'I want to hear more about you and your wedding. Tell me about happy things. Tell me about when you first realised Khalil loved you.' She smiled eagerly, like a child waiting for a story, sounding so certain of something Elena still wondered about.

Yet in that moment she knew she wanted to be like Dimah and believe. She wanted to hear and speak of happy things, to be certain that, no matter what happened with kingdoms or countries or thrones, she could be sure of her love for Khalil…and his love for her.

Gazing at Dimah's expectant face, Elena felt her own doubts begin to melt away. If Dimah could already see how Khalil loved her, then surely he did? Elena saw it in his eyes, felt it in his touch.

Maybe Khalil wasn't sure what love looked or felt like,

but Elena believed he loved her. She loved him. Nothing else mattered.

Nothing could change that.

Leaning forward, she began to tell Dimah all about how she and Khalil had fallen in love.

CHAPTER FOURTEEN

THE NEXT MORNING Elena came downstairs with Khalil to find Dimah standing in the centre of the salon. 'I need to talk to you,' she said, looking pale and resolute, and Khalil frowned.

'Dimah, what is it?'

'I need to tell you something.' Dimah closed the doors to the salon and turned to them, her fingers knotted anxiously together. 'I should have told you before, Khalil, a long time before. I never wanted to, but…' She trailed away, clearly nervous, and Khalil shook his head.

'I don't understand.'

Elena felt a sudden, terrible thrill of foreboding. She had a mad impulse to tell Dimah not to say anything. Not to change anything. Last night they'd all chatted and laughed over dinner, and then Khalil had taken Elena upstairs and made sweet love to her for half the night. She'd fallen asleep in his arms, perfectly content. Utterly secure in his feelings for her, and hers for him.

Yet now, standing there, looking at Dimah's anxious face, remembering her fretful pleas yesterday about Khalil forgetting Kadar, Elena's stomach knotted. Without even thinking about what she was doing, she flung out one hand.

'Don't.'

Khalil turned to stare at her incredulously. 'Do you know what she's going to say, Elena?'

'No, but…' What could she say? That she had some sort of premonition?

'But what? What do you know, Elena?' Khalil rounded on her and Elena blinked up, stunned at how quickly he had become suspicious, even angry. Dimah hadn't said anything, Elena didn't even know what she was going to say, yet here was Khalil, glaring at her accusingly.

'Khalil,' she whispered and he turned back to Dimah.

'What do you need to tell me, Dimah?'

'I should have told you a long time ago, Khalil.' For once Dimah's voice was low, certain, which made Elena all the more anxious. What was she going to say? 'Perhaps even when you were a boy, but I was afraid. Afraid first for you, and how you would take it, and then afraid for me. How you would feel about me keeping such a secret.'

Khalil stared at her, his expression shuttered. 'You are speaking in riddles.'

'Only because I am still afraid to tell you the truth,' Dimah admitted quietly. 'But I can see you have changed, Khalil. I know you love Elena—'

'Don't tell me what I feel.' Khalil cut her off brusquely and everything in Elena cringed and shrank. What was happening, and how had it all gone so wrong, so quickly?

Because it hadn't been strong enough to begin with.

'Khalil.' Dimah faced him directly, bravely, as if she were facing a firing squad—a death sentence. 'Hashem is not your father.'

His expression, amazingly, did not change. It did not so much as flicker. He didn't even blink.

'Say something,' Dimah said softly and a muscle in his jaw bunched.

'Nonsense.'

'You don't believe me?' Dimah blinked, incredulous.

'Why are you telling me this now, Dimah, after so many years?' He nodded towards Elena. 'Is it because of Elena? Because you think I've changed?'

Elena flinched; he sounded so contemptuous.

'Partly. You have more to live for now, Khalil, than being Sheikh.'

He clenched his hands into fists. 'But you're lying. Hashem is my father.'

Dimah cocked her head and in that moment Elena imagined the older woman was looking at Khalil as she had when he'd first come to her, wild and angry and so very terrified. 'Why would I lie, Khalil?'

He shrugged, the movement abrupt, aggressive. 'You never wanted me to return to Kadar. Maybe my marriage to Elena has given you the opportunity—'

'What opportunity? To deny you your birthright?'

'It *is* my birthright.'

'No,' Dimah said with heavy finality. 'It is not.'

Khalil shook his head. He held himself rigid, his gaze unblinking. '*No.*'

Everything in Elena ached as she realised what he was facing: the loss of his life's purpose, his very self. No wonder he wanted to deny it.

'I know it is a terrible thing for you to accept—'

'How can I accept it?' he demanded, and for a moment it seemed as if he almost wanted an answer to the question. 'Why would you not tell me for twenty-five years?'

'I told you, I was afraid!' Dimah's voice rang out, harsh and desperate. 'The more time passed, the more difficult it became. I did not want you to think badly of me, or your mother. Her memory seemed like the only thing that sustained you.'

'And you are tainting her memory now!' Elena saw the agony in his eyes. 'She was always so gentle with me. How could you do such a thing, Dimah? How could you accuse her of such a crime?'

'Oh, Khalil.' Dimah's voice broke. 'I'm a pitiful old woman, I know. I should have said something before. Long before. I closed my eyes to your ambition because I thought you would let go of it, in time. When Aziz became Sheikh, at least. I hoped that, in telling you now, I might finally set you free from this fruitless hope you've clung to for so long. That you'd be happy with the life you are making with Elena.'

'Why would my father make his will so open-ended, if I was not his son?' Khalil demanded.

'Maybe because Aziz has never seemed interested in Kadar,' Dimah offered helplessly. 'I don't know why, Khalil. But I do know what is true, and I'm sorry I didn't tell you sooner.'

Elena stepped forward and reached out one trembling hand. 'Khalil,' she began, but he jerked away from her.

'This suits you, doesn't it?' he said in a snarl. 'Now you'll have just what you wanted—a puppet prince at your beck and call.'

She blinked, stung. 'That's not fair. And that's not what I want at all.'

'It's certainly not what I want,' Khalil snapped. 'I'll never forget Kadar and my birthright and everything that has ever been important to me. Everything I've ever *been*.' His voice broke on the last word and he turned away from her, his head bowed.

'I'm sorry,' Dimah said quietly. 'I should have spoken before. I knew I had to speak now, since you were intending on returning to Kadar.'

'How would you even know such a thing as this? My mother—'

'Told me. She wrote me a letter, admitting everything. She even had a photograph of him, Khalil. Of your father.'

'*No.*' The one word was a cry of anguish and it broke Elena right open. Without even thinking of what she was doing or how Khalil might react, she went to him.

'Khalil.' She put her arms around his rigid body. 'Khalil.'

Tears started in her eyes. What could she say to him? How could she make this better?

'It can't be true,' Khalil said, and she heard then the agonised acceptance in his voice. He believed. He didn't want to believe, but he did.

'I can show you the letter, if you like,' Dimah said quietly. 'The photograph.'

Khalil gave a little shake of his head, then shrugged out of Elena's embrace, his back to them both. 'Who was he?' he asked, his voice barely audible.

'One of the palace guards,' Dimah answered in a whisper. 'You have his eyes.'

Khalil let out a sound that was almost a moan. Then he shook his head. 'I can't—' He stopped, stared blankly for a moment. 'I need to be alone,' he said, and walked out of the room without looking at either of them again.

It couldn't be true. *It couldn't, it couldn't, it couldn't.*

He sounded like a little boy, Khalil thought with a surge of fury. Like a terrified little boy, begging for mercy.

Don't hit me. Please don't hit me. Where is my mother? My father? Please...

The tears had run down his dirty face and Abdul-Hafiz had just laughed.

Now Khalil swore aloud and slammed his fist against the wall, causing a dent, bruising his hand and bloodying his knuckles.

It *couldn't* be true.

Yet he knew it was. And with that awful truth came the even more terrible realisation that everything he'd built his life on had been for nothing.

Every choice he'd made, every hope he'd had, had been for clearing his mother's name and claiming his legacy. His birthright. It had been who he was, and now that it had been taken away he was left spinning, empty, exposed. He had nothing. He *was* nothing.

He would not, would never, be Sheikh of Kadar.

Neither, he acknowledged with leaden certainty, would he be Elena's husband.

Elena paced the salon of Dimah's townhouse, her mind spinning, her heart aching. Khalil had left that morning, right after that awful confrontation, and although it was nearing midnight he had still not returned.

Dimah had gone to bed, after reassuring her that Khalil would return soon and things would look better in the morning. Elena had felt like shaking her. Things wouldn't look any better in the morning, not for Khalil. She knew what kind of man he was, how strong and proud. How he'd built everything on the foundation that the throne of Kadar was his by right. To have it taken away would devastate him…and he would be too proud to admit it.

And how would he be feeling, knowing that the man he'd thought was his father wasn't? That the truths he'd insisted on believing for so long, that had been sustaining him, were actually lies?

She longed to see him, to put her arms around him and comfort him. To tell him it didn't matter to her whether he was Sheikh or not. She didn't care who his parents were, or if he had a title. She wanted to tell him she loved him properly, not just hint at it. She wanted that love to make a difference.

And yet, deep down inside, she was afraid it wouldn't.

She heard the front door open and the slow, deliberate tread of a person who seemed utterly weary, even defeated. Elena hurried to the door, her heart thumping in her chest.

'Khalil.'

He turned to face her, the lines of his face haggard and yet his expression strangely, terribly blank.

'Elena. I didn't think you would still be awake.'

'Of course I'm awake!' she cried. 'I've been worried about you, Khalil, wondering how you are, how you're coping—'

'Coping?' He spoke the single word with contempt. 'Don't worry about me, Elena.'

'Of course I worry about you.' She bit her lip then took a deep breath. 'I love you, Khalil.'

He let out a hard laugh and Elena flinched. 'A little late for that, Elena.'

'Late? Why?'

'Because there is no reason for us to be married any more.'

'What?' Shock reverberated through her so her body practically vibrated with it. She stared at him in disbelief. 'No reason? Why is that, Khalil?'

He stared at her evenly, unmoved. 'You know why.'

'I know you no longer have a claim to the throne of Kadar. I know you've suffered a great disappointment. But I am still your wife. We're still *married*.'

'We'll get an annulment.'

'An annulment? How? We've made love, Khalil.'

'It can be done.'

She shook her head slowly, shock warring with hurt. Then both were replaced by a deep, hard anger. 'You coward,' she said, and her voice was cold. 'You selfish, thoughtless *coward*. You think because you have no need of me and our convenient marriage you can just forget your vows? Forget me?'

'How is this marriage convenient for you, Elena? I have no title, no claim. *I'm* the pretender. Do you think your Council will approve your marriage to me? Or will Markos just use it as a reason to depose you, consider it another foolish choice you've made?'

She blinked back tears. 'I don't care.'

'You should.'

'Forget my Council!' Elena cried. 'Forget our countries

or convenience. You told me you wanted to love me, Khalil. What happened to that? Did you decide you didn't want to any more? Or were you lying?' Her voice and body both shook as she demanded, 'Do you have no honour at all?'

'This isn't about honour,' Khalil retorted. 'I'm setting you free, Elena.'

'Setting me free? You haven't even asked if I want that kind of freedom. Don't hide behind excuses, Khalil. You're a better man than that.'

'Am I?' he demanded, his voice ringing in the sudden silence. 'Am I really, Elena? I don't even know what I am any more, if I am not my father's son. If I am not—' He drew a ragged breath. 'I've built my life on something that is a lie. Everything I've done, everything I've been…it's gone. So what am I now?'

'You are,' Elena said quietly, 'the man I love. I didn't fall in love with the Sheikh of Kadar, Khalil. I fell in love with the man who kissed my tears and held me in his arms. Who protected and encouraged and believed in me. I fell in love with that man.'

'And that man no longer exists.'

'He does.'

Khalil shook his head then stared at her openly, emptily. 'What am I going to do now, Elena? What purpose can I serve? Who can I even be?'

A tear trickled down Elena's cheek. 'You can be my husband, Khalil. You can be the Prince Consort of Thallia. You can be the father to our children.' He didn't answer, so she continued, her voice rising with determination. 'You can be the man you've always been, Khalil. A man with pride and strength and tenderness. A man who commands people's loyalty and who works hard for it. Why limit yourself? Why be defined by who sired you, or a title? There is so much more to you than that. So much more to *us*.'

She took a step towards him, her hands outstretched. 'Kadar is in your blood, Khalil. It's still your country, and you are still Sheikh of your own tribe. You told me you wanted to repair your country, and you still can. Aziz will need you to help him. Kadar needs you. People will look to you for the way forward, for peace.'

Khalil didn't talk for a long moment. Elena held her breath, hardly daring to hope, to believe…

To trust.

Now, more than ever, she needed to trust him. 'Khalil,' she said softly, his name a caress, a promise.

'Don't you even care?' he asked after an endless moment. 'Doesn't it matter to you that I'm no one now? I'm just some nameless bastard.'

And then she realised he needed to trust her as much as she needed to trust him. To trust her to love him, even now. Especially now. 'I told you, you're my husband, and I am your wife. It doesn't matter, Khalil. It doesn't matter at all.'

She saw a flicker of hope in his eyes, like the first light of dawn, then he shook his head. 'Your Council—'

'You told me I didn't need a husband to stand up to my Council, and I don't. I'm stronger now, Khalil. You've made me strong.' Another step, and she was touching him, her hand curling around his arm. 'But I need a husband to be my helpmate and equal. Someone I can love and support, who will love and support me. Standing side by side with me.'

Khalil closed his eyes briefly. 'I feel as if everything I've ever known, everything I've counted on, has been ripped away from me. Destroyed.'

'I haven't,' Elena said softly. 'I'm still here.'

He reached for her hand. 'After so many years of anger, I don't know what to feel now. My father had a right to banish me.'

'Did he? He could have treated you far more kindly than he did.'

'And my mother…'

'You don't know what her situation was, Khalil. How unhappy she was, or what drove her to it.'

He nodded slowly. Elena knew it would take a long time for him to find peace with these revelations,, but she wanted to help him

He turned to her, his eyes wide and bleak, his voice raw. 'I love you, Elena. I didn't think I even knew what love was, but you've showed me in so many ways. You've believed in me, trusted me even when I didn't deserve to have that trust. I still don't know if I do. I don't know what the future can look like,' he told her, a confession. 'I don't know how to *be*.'

'We'll figure it out together.' She stood in front of him, letting all her hope and love shine in her eyes. 'I love you, Khalil. And you love me. That's all that matters.'

His face crumpled for a second and then he pulled her into his arms. 'Oh, Elena,' he said, and he buried his face in her hair. 'Elena. I love you so much. I'm sorry for being a fool. For being afraid.'

'You think this doesn't scare me?' Elena answered with a wobbly laugh, and she felt Khalil's smile against her hair.

'Then maybe we'll be scared together.'

'That sounds good to me.'

Khalil's arms tightened around her. 'I don't deserve you.'

'I could say the same thing.'

He kissed her then, softly, and it was a kiss that held so much tenderness and love that her heart swelled. 'I still don't know what will happen. What—what the future looks like. I'll have to talk to Aziz, renounce my claim...'

'I know.'

'You're right. I can still help Kadar. I want to.'

'They need you, Khalil. I need you.'

He pressed his forehead against hers, his hands framing her face. 'I love you.'

She smiled against his palm. 'You told me that before, but I don't think I'll ever get tired of hearing it.'

'Me neither.'

'I love you, Khalil.'

He closed his eyes. 'I never thought I'd ever hear any-one say that to me.'

'I'll say it. I'll keep saying it.'

He kissed her again, pulling her even closer to him. 'Don't ever stop saying it, Elena. And I won't either. No matter what happens.'

'No matter what happens,' she promised.

Neither of them knew just what the future held. Khalil would need to grieve; they both needed to grow. And their love, Elena knew, would keep them strong.

* * * * *

If you enjoyed this book,
look out for Aziz's story in
COMMANDED BY THE SHEIKH
by Kate Hewitt.
Coming next month.

#3277 THE VALQUEZ BRIDE
The Playboys of Argentina
by Melanie Milburne
Untouched Theodora Marlstone always hoped for a fairy-tale wedding—instead she's facing a convenient marriage with playboy Alejandro Valquez. His eyes promise raw sensuality, not devotion, but seducing his buttoned-up bride proves a challenge Alejandro just can't resist!

#3278 THE UNCOMPROMISING ITALIAN
by Cathy Williams
With a threat that would expose his greatest secret, billionaire Alessio Baldini needs the expertise of beautiful Lesley Fox to make it stop. She is temptation personified—but mixing business and pleasure leads to one very lasting consequence....

#3279 PRINCE HAFIZ'S ONLY VICE
Royal & Ruthless
by Susanna Carr
Prince Hafiz swore to redeem his past sins and devote himself to his country. There's only one thing he loves more: his mistress, Lacey Maxwell. Lacey surrendered *everything* to be with her prince, but could their secret passion cost Hafiz his crown?

#3280 A DEAL BEFORE THE ALTAR
by Rachael Thomas
Georgina Henshaw will do anything for her younger sister—even marry a stranger! Her proposal is irresistible to Santos Ramirez, but the ruthless billionaire will have no paper marriage. His beautiful new wife *must* provide him with an heir...!

YOU CAN FIND MORE INFORMATION ON UPCOMING HARLEQUIN® TITLES, FREE EXCERPTS AND MORE AT WWW.HARLEQUIN.COM.

HPCNM0914RB

REQUEST YOUR
FREE BOOKS!

2 FREE NOVELS PLUS
2 FREE GIFTS!

YES! Please send me 2 FREE Harlequin Presents® novels and my 2 FREE gifts (gifts are worth about $10). After receiving them, if I don't wish to receive any more books, I can return the shipping statement marked "cancel." If I don't cancel, I will receive 6 brand-new novels every month and be billed just $4.30 per book in the U.S. or $4.99 per book in Canada. That's a saving of at least 14% off the cover price! It's quite a bargain! Shipping and handling is just 50¢ per book in the U.S. and 75¢ per book in Canada.* I understand that accepting the 2 free books and gifts places me under no obligation to buy anything. I can always return a shipment and cancel at any time. Even if I never buy another book, the two free books and gifts are mine to keep forever.

106/306 HDN FVRK

Name
(PLEASE PRINT)

Address
Apt. #

City   State/Prov.   Zip/Postal Code

Signature (if under 18, a parent or guardian must sign)

Mail to the **Harlequin®** Reader Service:
IN U.S.A.: P.O. Box 1867, Buffalo, NY 14240-1867
IN CANADA: P.O. Box 609, Fort Erie, Ontario L2A 5X3

Are you a current subscriber to Harlequin Presents books and want to receive the larger-print edition?
Call 1-800-873-8635 or visit www.ReaderService.com.

* Terms and prices subject to change without notice. Prices do not include applicable taxes. Sales tax applicable in N.Y. Canadian residents will be charged applicable taxes. Offer not valid in Quebec. This offer is limited to one order per household. Not valid for current subscribers to Harlequin Presents books. All orders subject to credit approval. Credit or debit balances in a customer's account(s) may be offset by any other outstanding balance owed by or to the customer. Please allow 4 to 6 weeks for delivery. Offer available while quantities last.

Your Privacy—The Harlequin® Reader Service is committed to protecting your privacy. Our Privacy Policy is available online at www.ReaderService.com or upon request from the Harlequin Reader Service.

We make a portion of our mailing list available to reputable third parties that offer products we believe may interest you. If you prefer that we not exchange your name with third parties, or if you wish to clarify or modify your communication preferences, please visit us at www.ReaderService.com/consumerchoice or write to us at Harlequin Reader Service Preference Service, P.O. Box 9062, Buffalo, NY 14269. Include your complete name and address.